Sins and Sacrifices

by

I0634219

Dorinda D. E. Nusum

Published by
DoriNu Publications, LLC
Dayton, OH
www.dorindadenusum.com

Published by DORINU PUBLICATIONS, LLC
DoriNu Publications, LLC
Dayton, OH
DorindaDENusum.com

ISBN-13: 9780983566236
ISBN-10: 0983566232

Printed in the United States of America

DEDICATION

For my parents, Madelyn Harvey and the Late
Eugene Nusum

~

Without you, there would be no me! Thanks for
giving me life, love, and many years of happiness!

Acknowledgements

Special thanks first and foremost to God who has blessed me with many talents that have proven fruitful and self-fulfilling.

To my husband, Demetrius, my biggest fan, thanks for reading and re-reading and for helping me to get a kick-start. I love you.

To my children, Deonte, Jayden, and Geneia- I want you to be as proud of me as I am of you. You are my sweethearts!

Thanks also to my parents Madelyn Harvey-Elliott and the Late Eugene Nusum who collectively taught me to think, to feel, and to love.

To my siblings, Sharmaine and Marlin, my second biggest fans. Thanks for providing the fuel for my literary fire.

To my wonderful family and friends in Bermuda for their ongoing support and dedication to each of my causes. You have been the wind beneath my wings from the very beginning and I know you'll be there helping me to fly higher as I continue to soar to success.

To my mother-in-law, Ernestine Grigsby for becoming an instant fan and for putting my name out there.

To my extended family, the staff of Montgomery County Juvenile Detention in Dayton, Ohio, thanks for showing me love and encouraging me through the infant stages of my writing.

Chapter 1 - Christine

I checked my makeup in my bedroom mirror. While I smacked my lips, smoothing out my lipstick, my husband, Deacon Charles Rutherford, stepped out of the bathroom, adjusting his tie.

"We'd better hurry or we'll be late. Service starts at eleven, Christine, not eleven-thirty." He said in a gruff and satirical manner. "And why are you wearing such a bright shade of lipstick? The last thing I need is for my wife to be looking like she's some kin to Jezebel. For Christ's sake, Chris, take some of that trash off your face."

I didn't answer. Instead, I looked repulsively at my husband in the mirror. His five foot eleven inch muscular frame, which was once strikingly handsome to me, had turned pudgy. His smooth even toned brown complexion, which once reminded me of creamy milk chocolate, was now pimpled and patchy, and the smile that Charles wore on his face that used to warm my heart was now almost non-existent.

Every morning for the past two years, I have questioned the reason I've remained married to

Charles. The first five years of our marriage was great. Charles fully catered to my every need, my every desire. While we were courting, Charles went through grave measures to win me over even though I, being a preacher's kid, was a tough catch. It was the thrill of the chase that I credit as the precise reason Charles fought so hard to win me over. Charles loves a challenge, and landing me was just the kind of boost his ego needed.

For the sake of keeping up appearances, Charles treated me superbly during our first year of marriage. He added additional rooms to our already lavish home on Brentwood Avenue, a Florida room, a larger bath, two extra guest rooms, extended the patio, and turned the attic into a luxurious loft, a hideaway created especially for me. He often invited our widowed Pastor, Reverend Conrad Baxter, to dinner, along with my father, Reverend John Bixby, my mother, Vernelle, and members of the Deacon Board and their wives. Our home was always filled with laughter and fellowship. Charles used to take advantage of every opportunity to brag about my delicious meals, the new outfits he'd purchased for me, new and expensive items we'd purchased for our home, and the amount of money we had unselfishly donated to charity.

I would be at his side blushing, flattered, but somewhat embarrassed. I thought the way my husband crowed about me and our life was charming, but I hated it when he would go overboard. My mother thought Charles was a first-rate husband, but my father never trusted Charles completely. He would raise his brow at Charles,

—

glance at him sideways and grunt "humph" with every statement Charles made while my mother would gently jab him in the ribs, and scold him sweetly.

From the second year of our marriage onward, things gradually started to change. Charles became too busy to host dinners, too tired to eat dinner with me, too cheap to buy me anything new, and too inattentive to know how to meet my needs, whether basic or emotional. I have never understood what brought about the changes in my husband. I suspect infidelity, but I have no proof of that, and I've considered his health, but Charles is too stubborn to see a doctor.

Whenever I try to talk with Charles about the way things are between the two of us, he retorts, "Why can't you leave me alone, woman? A woman is not supposed to nag her husband the way you do."

I often sit in our room for hours, crying or sleeping off my pain. Charles pretends he doesn't notice.

"You hear me woman? Wipe that garbage off your face and let's get a move on. It's almost ten forty-five. It takes twenty minutes to get to church. I'm gonna have to speed and pray to God I don't get caught. The devil is always trying to deter things, and this morning he's using my wife. Well I'm not having it," he continued to yell.

Charles snatched up his jacket and his car keys. He'd forgotten his Bible. It was on their nightstand, in the exact same spot it had been resting since last Sunday. I went to the table to pick it up, but decided to leave it instead. I went to the bathroom and grabbed a wet rag. I held back my

—

6

tears while I wiped the lipstick off my face completely. My knees started to buckle just as the car horn blew. I gathered my things as quickly as I could and headed out the door.

Charles sped out of our gate. He hated to be late for church. His image was everything. He wouldn't have it said that someone as dedicated to the church and as devoted to God as himself would arrive at the house of the Lord a minute past due.

Charles whipped into the church gate at exactly ten fifty-seven. With three minutes remaining, he yanked the keys out of the ignition and dashed out of the car. He was near the entrance before he turned back and realized I was tagging far behind. He shot me a scowl that made me quicken my pace.

Once I met him at the entrance, we went inside arm in arm. Charles greeted everyone with a smile and gently rubbed my back as he spoke to people and shook their hands on the way to our seats. I also smiled, camouflaging my true feelings. I felt like my own Judas.

Just as Charles and I took our seats, the choir marched in behind us singing Kirk Franklin's "Stomp". Charles laid his belongings on the pew, stood to his feet, and started stomping right along with them. He clapped his hands, danced, and had a Holy Ghost time.

I, determined not to let the devil bring me down this morning, laid my things down beside me, rose to my trembling feet, and sang with the choir. I clapped my hands gently, but before the song was over, I found myself slapping my hands together so roughly that they turned red and started to sting.

Charles watched me in awe. He hadn't seen me so passionately involved in the service in a long time. I could tell that he began to feel uncomfortable. I noticed that his clapping was suddenly off beat, beads of sweat streamed down his face, and he held tightly to the pew in front of us as if the room started to spin and he was trying to maintain his balance. He sat down. It was my turn to pretend I didn't notice. I smiled and suddenly, I felt a surge of energy, a taste of victory.

"Thank you, Jesus," I whispered under my breath. I continued to sing, praise, stomp, and clap. I didn't care how raw my hands felt. I was determined not to give in to the devil today.

The choir slowed down its pace. They sang "His Eye Is On The Sparrow," one of my favourite songs. While most of the congregation took their seats and hummed along, something got a hold of me and I stayed on my feet. They were feeling sturdier now.

With my eyes closed and with fervor I sang from the words "Why should I feel discouraged..." on down to "...And I know He watches over me." I know that song all too well. It has comforted me and carried me through many dreadful days.

When the song was over, I opened my eyes and realized I was the only one standing. More eyes were focused on me than on the choir. Charles was glaring, the preacher was smiling an uncomfortable smile, and members of the church were staring at me suspiciously. I felt a myriad of emotions: invigoration, triumph, shame, and fear. I slowly sat down. Charles turned his attention to-

—

wards the pastor whose expression seemed to imply he knew something wasn't right with me. I looked over at Charles. His hands were shaking. When he realized I was aware of them, he clasped his hands together to keep anyone else from noticing I suppose. I couldn't control myself. I grinned and prayed that God would forgive my maliciousness. I felt victorious again.

Janice, the I-think-I-am-too-cute-for-myself church secretary, read the announcements. Lydia Bohler sang a solo. The offering was collected and the choir director prayed over the funds. My favourite part of the service was soon to begin. Ever since I was a little girl, it was hearing the sermons that I loved the most about attending church. I used to sit in the living room and watch my daddy rehearse his Sunday speeches. He would pace back and forth and speak with force and intensity. His passion was spellbinding. Reverend Baxter, though only a few years older than I am, reminds me of my daddy. I loved his voice. I hate to admit it, but I have a slight crush on Reverend Baxter. In my mind, there is no man more attractive than a heartfelt man of God.

Reverend Baxter rose to speak. The entire congregation stood respectfully and gave him their undivided attention.

"Good Morning, Brothers and Sisters. It warms my heart to see so many of you out this morning. I'm sure the devil tried to hold you down. I'm sure something tried to block your path, but you made it here this morning by the grace of God. Welcome one and all. Please take your seats. Open your Bibles if you will to the book of Hebrews.

Today's lesson is on Faith. By FAITH and by FAITH alone did many of our Biblical brothers and Sisters overcome. Let's take a look at Moses. Moses mother put him into a basket and placed her son in the ocean on FAITH that someone of clean heart would find him and spare him. She trusted God to protect her child. Look at Sarah. It was only by FAITH that the barren woman received the strength she needed to conceive a child when she was past due. It was by FAITH that Abraham offered Isaac up to God as a sacrifice. Abraham had FAITH that God would raise his son up from the dead if only he obeyed and trusted Him. I could go on and on with my list of examples, but what I want you to hear more clearly than anything today is that you need to exercise your faith. No matter your circumstance, no matter what comes your way, you can handle it. We are too eager today to give up. We raise our hands and surrender at the first sight of pressure. This happens with our finances, in our families, in our marriages, in dealing with our children, in the workplace, and sometimes even with each other right here in the church."

There was a synchronized "umm humph" from the congregation. Women were cutting eyes, nodding heads, waving their hands in the air, patting down their weaves, and shouting, "Amen", "You tell 'em Pastor."

Reverend Baxter was fueled by their response. His pace quickened, his volume increased and he started walking around. He paced in front of his pew. He made his way down the aisle. He touched heads while he talked. He sought offenders while he walked. He was on a Christ led mission.

Reverend Baxter walked over to the pew where Charles and I sat. He reached his hand out to me. I gladly took his hand in mine. A sensation filtered through my body.

"Child," he said, "God is watching you. Though right now ye are of little faith, God wants you to hold firm to Him. He wants you to believe Him for miracles. He wants you to remember that it was He who made you. "Be still," he says, "...and know that I am God." There are going to be changes in your life. Be on the look out for them and thank God for each and every one, those you understand, and those you don't. Walk by faith, dear one, and not by sight. Walk by faith."

My hand started to tremble just as Reverend Baxter let it go. He patted me on the head and continued walking, talking, singing out his sermon, and spitting out verses. The congregation quickly turned their attention from me and focused on our leader. Everyone wanted something to hold onto. They remained attentive, waiting to grasp the bit of prophecy that belonged only to them.

Charles kept his head down and his eyes on his watch. He couldn't believe time was moving so slowly. He also couldn't believe how hot it was in the sanctuary this morning. Usually, the air was on full blast, but this morning, Charles felt the heat. As beads of sweat continued to roll down his face, Charles looked around. I'm sure he wanted to see if anyone else was sweating too. No one appeared to feel the heat. What had become my Heaven had turned into Charles's hell.

"Christine," Charles whispered to me. "You got any Tums in your purse?"

"No. I didn't bring them this morning. I left them in the medicine cabinet. You alright?" He didn't look good at all, so I was genuinely concerned now. I couldn't remember the last time I saw Charles looking so vulnerable.

"My stomach feels funny," he told me.

"What do you mean *funny*?" I asked him.

"It just don't feel right. Like it's tying up in knots or something."

"Do you want to leave?"

Charles really did want to go, but he didn't want anyone to think he left because he couldn't deal with the message.

"No. I'll sit here a while longer. You got any mints or anything?"

I reached into my purse and pulled out two peppermint discs.

"Here, try these."

The mints seemed to help Charles a little, but I could still see his discomfort. I thought of asking him again about leaving, but decided I wouldn't dare interfere if God were working on him.

Instead, I focused my attention on Reverend Baxter and I glanced at Charles from the corner of my eye every now and then. Throughout the entire service, Charles squirmed, fanned, checked his watch, and monitored the exit.

When service was over, women flocked to me, offering to keep me in their prayers, and telling me to give them a call if I should need anything. A few of them shot glares at Charles. Others smiled dryly at him and shook his hand limply. I had a good time talking to and hugging each of them.

Charles, on the other hand, was ready to go

"I'll be in the car," he told me.

"I'll be right there, Charles," I answered.

I spent ten more minutes talking with the ladies. It had been so long since I had socialized with them. I invited several of them over for lunch next week. I couldn't trust all of them, so I whispered invitations to those I deemed more genuine.

Just as I said my last goodbye to the ladies, Reverend Baxter approached me.

"Sis. Rutherford, it's so nice to see you again. How have you been?" He raised his brow on the word *been* indicating he wanted the truth.

"I'm doing fine, Pastor," I lied. "It just comes a time when a woman starts reflecting on her life, and it's at that precise moment that the devil tries to distort the details. I'll be fine though. I just need a moment to get myself together." I grinned, pleased that someone cared and also because I was admiring the beauty that was before me. I felt a tad bit guilty, but not enough to cause me to seek anybody's confessional.

"Well, Sis. You know you're not alone. Any time you need to talk, you know where to find me. That's not an empty invitation. That's what I'm here for. Call. If you need anything at all, just call."

I knew Reverend Baxter's invitation was sincere. Our eyes were fixed on each other, and we held hands for a moment longer. I was the first to break away. That made me feel good.

"Thank you," I whispered, "I'll remember that."

I turned and slowly walked out of the sanctuary on steady feet and with my head held high. I tried desperately to control a grin that just wouldn't leave my face. There was a new found joy in my heart.

I went outside slowly, not yet ready to confront my reality. Charles was waiting impatiently in the car. He was sitting in the passenger side with the windows rolled down and he was fanning himself with the church program. The parking lot was clear aside from one or two cars that belonged to the ushers.

"What took you so long, Christine? You were the first one out of your seat and now you're the last one out the door. You know I been sitting out here. You're just plain inconsiderate. You always been inconsiderate. You know my stomach's paining me and you got the nerve to be inside chatting it up and carrying on." He sucked his teeth. "You ain't got good sense nohow."

"I was talking to Reverend Baxter," I told him.

Charles held his stomach. "Drive, Christine, I need to get home. I think I'm catching a virus or something."

I looked at my husband and that uncontrollable grin emerged again.

"Why you grinning like a Cheshire, woman?" Charles snapped. I stopped trying to control my grin and let it turn into a full blown smile. I put the key in the ignition, cranked up the car and pulled out of the parking lot slowly. I caught a glimpse of Reverend Baxter in my rearview mirror. I put my hand out the window and waved goodbye to him. My smile stretched across my face. I looked over at Charles who was balled up and leaning in his seat. I drove the long way home.

Chapter 2 - Christine

Two weeks passed. Things between Charles and I were growing progressively worse and I was as confused as ever as to the reason for my husband's dissatisfaction with me. I continually asked Charles to sit with me to discuss our situation. Each time, Charles brusquely declined the offer.

Night after night, Charles would come home from work late, crawl into bed, turn his back to me, and start snoring within minutes. No conversation. No excuses. No passion.

My whimpering became my nightly lullaby. As I lay still, waiting for Charles to come home nights, many thoughts went through my mind, most of which centered around packing my bags and leaving Charles, but I don't think I'm emotionally or financially strong enough to survive on my own. I hate myself for that. Things between Charles and me need to change. I can't continue my marriage to Charles in the fashion to which he seemed to have become accustomed. First thing in the morning, I will demand that Charles sit and talk with me, and if he couldn't handle talking, I would be sure he would at least be forced to listen.

I rolled over and looked at the clock. It was two thirty-six. Charles usually woke at around seven. I eased out of bed and reached for my slippers and robe. "Thank God for moonlight", I whispered. I tiptoed out of the bedroom. On my way, a few of the wooden floorboards creaked, trying to squeal on me. I froze in position, nervous that Charles would wake.

Each time the floor creaked, I waited a couple of seconds before making another attempt at a trouble-free escape. I finally made it down the stairs, past the living room and to the kitchen. Relying heavily upon the moonlight for support, I hunted the kitchen for Charles's car keys. He usually hung them on the hook near the kitchen entrance, but they weren't there tonight. I searched the countertops. The keys were not there either, so I decided to quash Plan A.

I opened the drawer that contained the sharp utensils and pulled out a knife. I felt the blade. "Umm," I mumbled, "This one will do." I unlocked the kitchen door and turned the knob carefully. Then, I opened the door as though it were heavy, and quietly stepped outside. I shut the door behind me. It gave a thud. I jumped and my heart beat fast. I waited for a minute. I looked up at the bedroom window and waited for the light to come on. It didn't. Charles hadn't heard.

I looked around my neighbourhood. Everything was quiet and still. I'd watched an episode of COPS before going to bed tonight, so now

I was paranoid that some deranged loony would be waiting to pounce on an unsuspecting victim and that tonight it would be my turn.

I've been begging Charles to fix the garage door so that we wouldn't be forced outside to get into our vehicles, especially with winter coming, but Charles just grunts and ignores my requests.

I said a quick prayer as I made my way around the bend of the house to the driveway. I passed by my white Honda Civic and went straight towards Charles's black Mercedes Benz. I hadn't paid too much attention to our cars before. *Black and white*, I thought. *Just like us, night and day.* I shook my head.

I bent down and rubbed my hand over Charles's rear tire on the right side. I felt for a groove, and prayed, "Dear Father, forgive me for what I am about to do." With my last word, I plunged my knife into Charles's tire. I heard a light whistling sound. I felt powerful. That gave me the confidence I needed to continue. I went around to the other side and punctured the other tire. I then went to the front of the car and continued my vandalism. The car whistled out a tune that made me smile. I held my knife high and cut circles in the air with it. I did a victory dance. My nerves had subsided and my plan was well under way.

I made my way back inside. I eased in the same way I eased out, re-tracing each of my steps until she made it to the kitchen. As I stood there in the dark, returning the knife to it's resting place, I heard a sound that made me jump out of my skin. I slammed the knife drawer and caught my finger. I wanted to cry out of pain, but more out of fear.

"Whatchu been doing, woman? Why you bin outside?" Charles insisted upon knowing. Even though it was dark, I could see Charles squinting at me. I suddenly felt ill. I tried to think of something to say, some explanation to give Charles that would suit him until I was ready to proceed with the next part of my plan, but nothing would come to mind. Instead, I hung my head and said nothing.

Charles walked up to me slowly. It was plain to see that the Devil had taken over my husband's body. I trembled, and remained focused on the floor.

"You hear me talkin' to you, woman? Why you bin outside? Whatchu been doin' out there? You hidin' somebody out there? Huh? Are you? You got you somebody outside?"

I quickly raised my head; astounded that Charles would think such a thing. "Of course I ain't got anybody outside, Charles. As long as we been married I ain't as much as looked at anybody else." At that moment, anyone listening would have probably expected the word "massa" to come out of my mouth. I sounded like a slave trying to dodge a whooping.

"Then what would a woman be doing out doors at almost three o'clock in the morning? What purpose would a decent woman have for that?" Charles was squinting harder now and his voice was more demanding.

I didn't answer. There was no immediate explanation that I could give that would sound reasonably just. As I stood there, trying to conjure a defense, Charles grabbed me by the arm and tossed me across the kitchen. He reached into the junk drawer and pulled out a flashlight. He turned it on and shone it directly into my petrified face. Without saying a word, Charles opened the kitchen door and went outside. I got weak in the knees and slid down the wall that had been kind enough to hold me up.

"Oh, my God," I said, "Oh, Dear God."

Within seconds, I could hear Charles stomping back to the house. His footsteps deafened me as he made his way closer to the kitchen door. He slammed the door shut and locked it. He came over to me, gripped me up off the floor and threw me against the wall.

"Woman, you done it this time. I have had enough. You done messed up this time." Charles wrapped his large, heavy, hand around my neck and landed a quick blow to my face with the other. One blow led to another, and another, until my cries got louder and my body became limp. Charles let go of me. I fell to the floor. He left me there and heartlessly went upstairs.

I mustered enough strength to touch my face. I felt blood on my cheek. I lay on the floor, confused, physically hurt, and emotionally wounded. I couldn't figure out how the man who had once wooed me had transformed himself into such a monster. There were no warning signs given for the way Charles attitude and behaviour had changed.

I decided I didn't care anymore about seeking an explanation for Charles's actions. I just knew it was time to toughen up. I couldn't afford to be weak anymore. I was no one's doormat, so I wouldn't allow Charles to walk all over me anymore.

I had stood for Charles's disregard far longer than I should have, but there was no way I would tolerate his beatings. Things were escalating out of control. The thought of what lay ahead for me made me feel drained. I rested my head on the floor, my pillow for the next few hours.

Charles made his way to the kitchen at his usual time, six thirty a.m. He ignored the fact that I was still lying on the floor partially awake and too numb to move. He stepped over me and made his way to the refrigerator to pack himself a carry out breakfast. I lay on the cold tile still amazed that my once loyal and loving husband had become such a bitter brute.

I slowly lifted my head off the floor. I looked up at Charles who I could tell was watching me from the corner of his eye. He put his lunch into a wrinkled brown paper sack, took his thermos bottle out of the refrigerator, and picked up his coat.

"I'll be home at the usual time," he told me in a muffled but sorrowful tone.

I didn't say a word. Instead, I nodded my head to acknowledge that I had heard. When I did, I felt stiffness in my neck. I put my hand on the injured spot. Charles noticed.

"You made me hit you last night, Christine. You shouldnt've messed with my car. You had no right," Charles justified. He reached out to help me to my feet. I flinched. I was sure he was ready for round two. When saw it was safe, I reluctantly took his hand. Charles looked at my eye again and hung his head. He pointed to the evidence of his fury.

"Put some ice on that." He told me

sympathetically. "Im'a need your car, of course."

Without waiting for a response, Charles took my car keys off the key holder on the wall and left.

Charles spent his days working in the soup kitchen downtown, doing hospital visitations, and helping out at Bright Side Nursing Home. The church financial committee deemed him one of their greatest assets and paid him handsomely. He also went on tours, visiting sister churches once every three months. They often took up love offerings that lined his pockets well. I used to go on his ventures with him, but lately, Charles has insisted upon going alone.

In the meantime, I play the pristine wife. I cook, clean, dust, make craft items and read my Bible. Sometimes I go out into the garden and put together bouquets of flowers for church members or neighbours who are sick. Even though I often find fulfillment in my daily tasks, I am beginning to feel more and more like I need to do more with my life. I wish Charles would let me accompany him again. I believe that would lift my spirits and possibly improve my marriage. Sometimes I think that maybe I'm not assertive enough with Charles. Maybe that's why he treats me the way he does.

I went upstairs to the master bathroom and took a close look at my eye in the mirror.

"Nothing a little makeup can't hide," I said to myself.

I dug through the closet and pulled out a cosmetics bag that contained a few tubes of lipstick, some blush, and liquid foundation, items I used often before Charles and I were married. I rather like the way I look in makeup, but Charles always chastises me for wearing it. Because I couldn't totally part with my beauty products, I keep a few well-hidden pieces in seclusion. The liquid foundation would come in handy today.

I washed my face well with Noxzema, taking extra special care to softly massage my painfully bruised eye. Then, I applied the foundation, putting extra on the area that needed the most covering. I smiled when I was done. My bruise was hardly visible. I decided to also put on a little lipstick. My face was becoming radiant. *With just a little blush*, I thought, *I would look absolutely beautiful.*

I stepped back from the mirror and looked at the face staring back at me. I smiled again. Suddenly, I felt invigorated. I went to the closet and searched for my red dress with the white flowers covering the shoulders. I hunted through my drawers for a pair of taupe pantyhose, and then went to the closet again to retrieve my overpriced red pumps. I started to hum.

As I dressed, the phone rang. I checked the caller ID. It was Myrna, one of the choir members. She usually called to fill me in on the latest gossip, and although I knew it was a sin, I would often indulge. I was tempted to answer the phone, but today, I had more important business that needed tending to. I ignored the ringing and continued to dress.

I found my red and white purse and transferred my belongings from my brown one into it. I looked in the full-length mirror at myself. I looked at the front, both sides, and the back. I was stunning. I hurried downstairs to the kitchen in search of my car keys.

I must have been searching for almost fifteen minutes before I remembered that Charles had taken my car. I straightened my slouching shoulders and took up my purse. I wouldn't allow anything to ruin my plans. I went back upstairs and took some change out of Charles's coin bank. I needed enough for a round trip bus ride. I decided to take enough to cover lunch as well.

I looked at the clock. It was 8:47 a.m. The bus that traveled to the downtown area usually made it outside of my house at approximately 9:00a.m. I went downstairs, took up Charles's keys, locked the house, and dashed to the bus stop. I didn't want to take a chance at missing my public provided ride. While I sat on the bench waiting, several of my neighbours passed by and waved. All of them gave me a smile that confirmed that I looked good. Mrs. Kellick was walking her dog, Mr. Mohan had come out to retrieve the morning paper, and Miss Bellue was in her yard tending to the weeds. I confidently raised my hand and waved at each of them. I even enquired about their agendas for the day. When they asked about mine, I proudly told them that I had some important issues to handle that required my immediate attention.

The bus came. I got on, paid the fare, and sat in the seat nearest the driver.

I hadn't ridden a bus in ages, so I was somewhat nervous about the ride.

It took twenty minutes before the bus arrived at the downtown depot. I looked around at the hustlers and bustlers. I smelled the sweet stench of exhaust, and I stood for a minute, trying to identify the various sounds around me that created the type of harmonious racket one would only find in the city. It took me a minute to get my bearings. I was within walking distance to the Brightside Nursing Home, and it was only 9:27a.m. Charles would still be there.

My journey was longer than I thought and my blistering feet ached by the time I made it to the Home. *I should've worn flats*, I thought.

I opened the door to Brightside and walked down the hall past all of the administrative offices and entered the dining hall.

"Chrissy," called out Maria, the Mexican housekeeper. "It's been a long time. Where chu bin highting?"

I hugged her like she was my long lost sister. "It's good to see you, Maria. I've been at home, tending to matters there, but since my work has wound down a bit…"

"Chu dawt chu woot come down here and see jore ole friends," Maria interrupted. "How's Charlie been?"

I frowned. "Charles? What do you mean?" I asked, trying not to sound suspicious.

"Well, eez bin so lonk since I seen Charlie, I was wantering how eez bin." Maria told me.

"Have you been on vacation, Maria?" I asked her, hoping to God she had been.

Maria looked puzzled. Then she laughed. "Facation? No, no, no. Maria can't afford no facation, Honey. Maria has seven kids jew remember? Maria must work, work, work. All de time Maria works."

"And you haven't seen Charles," I asked. This time, suspicion uncontrollably took over my tone.

"Honey, Charles no bin here. Last time I see Charles was,...I tone no when. Jew still marry to Charles?"

My eyes watered. I really didn't know how to answer that question. It was becoming more and more apparent that Charles and I had no marriage at all.

"I no mean to upset you, Chrissy. Jew okay?"

"I'm fine," I told her. "I guess Charles's neglecting to tell me he doesn't come here to work anymore crossed his mind. He's been so preoccupied lately," I lied.

I hugged Maria, briefly asked about her kids and about her husband, Manuel and said goodbye to her. I wanted to ask Maria the reason Charles hadn't been working at Brightside anymore, but I was feeling embarrassed enough for the moment. Instead, I hurried out of the building before I would bump into anyone else. I wasn't up for any more conversation.

As soon as I made it outside, I clutched my chest. I felt like I couldn't breathe. With tears rolling down my cheeks, I stomped back to the bus station. It's a good thing I had taken some extra change. There was another stop I needed to make before heading home.

I looked around for the bus to Huntington Square. It was roaring and ready to go. The driver had just shut the door when I ran to it and knocked. I made it on, paid the fare, and this time, found a seat near the middle. I wanted to blend in this time. I stared out the window the entire ride, but I didn't notice any of the scenery. All I could think about was how distant Charles and I had become, how our marriage was steadily dissipating.

The bus ride to Huntington Square lasted only fifteen minutes, but it felt like an hour. I walked two blocks to the soup kitchen located in Kingdom Hall. I stomped past everyone, nodding and smiling and saying quick hellos. Everyone was staring at me strangely. I suspected the reason was because I was usually far more cordial. I would make apologies later. For now, I had to find Charles.

I knocked on the door to the kitchen before letting myself in. Jonathan Bolling was the first person I saw.

"Jonathan. Hi. Where's Charles? Has he made it in yet?" I asked the twenty four year old culinary volunteer.

"Hey, Mrs. Rutherford, nice to see you again. No, I haven't seen Mr. Rutherford. Are you expecting him in today?" he asked me cheerily while wiping what appeared to be spaghetti sauce all over his apron.

"Well, yes," I answered, "Aren't you?"

"No, ma'am. Mr. Rutherford only comes in on Tuesdays and Thursdays. Today is Monday," he told me. He furrowed his brow. I was messed up in the head now, but I had to play it off.

"Of course, silly me. What am I thinking? Anyway, how have you been?"

Jonathan answered, but I didn't hear a word of what he said.

"What happened to your eye, Mrs. Rutherford?" Jonathan asked.

"Huh?" I answered.

"Your eye. What happened?"

I had forgotten about my eye. My day couldn't

get much worse than this. My husband's gone AWOL and now I have to stand here and explain my beat up and blackened eye to a kid.

"Oh, yes, my eye. Well, Jonathan, that's what fumbling around in the dark will get you. I feel so stupid. It must look terrible."

"Nah," Jonathan said, "not too bad. Anyway, Mrs. Rutherford, it was nice seeing you, but I'd better get back to the kitchen. The lunch crowd will be here before long."

As soon as Jonathan left, I dug in my purse for my compact the way a drug addict would scrounge for his crack. I looked in the mirror. My bruise had been completely revealed and my tears had made stains in my makeup.

"Oh, dear God," I said to myself, "no wonder everyone was staring at me." Humiliation was making friends with me today, my sidekick. As tears formed in my eyes for the second time in less than an hour, I tried to wipe them away before anyone else noticed. I needed to put concealor on my eye, but before I managed to do so, someone tapped me on the shoulder.

"Sister Rutherford. I wouldn't have expected to see you here today, but how nice it is for you to show up. Did you come to help out?"

It was Reverend Baxter. I parted my lips in an attempt to answer, but only a whimper came out. I had no choice; I surrendered and let my tears flow freely. Reverend Baxter reached for my hand and led me out of the dining hall through the back entrance.

"Christine," he said, voice soft and compassionate, "What's the matter? I could tell you haven't been yourself for some time now. I'm worried about you."

I wanted so desperately to take that man in my arms. I needed so much to be held. Instead, I held on tight to Reverend Baxter's hand. It was soft and warm, yet strong and protecting.

"I'm alright, Reverend, or at least I will be. Please forgive me. I didn't mean to break down the way I did. I'm so embarrassed." I told him.

"Christine, what happened to your eye?" he asked me.

"Oh, I ugh…I…" I had a harder time lying to Reverend Baxter than I did lying to Jonathan. "You see, I…"

Reverend Baxter put his hand on my chin and tilted my head slightly. "Did your husband do this to you?" he asked.

I didn't' answer, but my tears did, loudly and clearly.

"You don't need to say a word," Reverend Baxter told me. He had a look of disgust on his face that I had never seen before.

"Where are you headed, Chris?"

Reverend Baxter had never addressed me so informally before.

His calling me Chris warmed me a little.

"Home," was all I could say.

"Please, allow me to walk you to your car," he offered. Are you parked out front?"

"No. Actually…" I hesitated, "I umm…I took the bus here." "What's happened to your car?" Reverend Baxter asked.

"Charles needed it today." I told him. I could hear a tremor in my voice. The Reverend raised his brow the same way Jonathan had when he asked about my eye. He wanted some type of explanation, but I wouldn't dare provide him with one.

"What happened to…Never mind, that's not my business. In that case, won't you please allow me the privilege of driving you home?"

I nodded. Reverend Baxter led the way to his car.

He drove through the city, but the drive felt more like a country ride. I felt at ease, and welcome.

Every now and then, I snuck glances at the Reverend. I pretended I was his wife and that I was sitting on the right hand side of the man I loved. I wanted to lay my head on the Reverend's shoulder the way I used to do whenever Charles drove me. Instead, I used the headrest. It only took a minute before I fell asleep.

While I slept, I dreamt that Reverend Baxter was sneaking glances at me. He thought of how wonderful it would be if I were his wife instead of Charles's. He whispered to himself that I was a fine woman, a total proverbial package. He went on to say that he missed Brenda, his wife, and he thought he would never find another woman that he would fall in love with, but then he met me. He prayed over his feelings for me, for the lust that was forming in his heart. He told God that he didn't want to violate any of the commandments, but he found himself often coveting his neighbour's wife. He asked God to work with him on that. I could feel myself smiling.

I was still asleep by the time Reverend Baxter made it to my house. He drove up and parked right next to Charles's car. He must have noticed Charles tires as soon as he pulled into the driveway. I heard him mumble, "A*ll four tires flat, hmm.*" I kept my eyes closed. I didn't want to have to answer to his query. To my surprise, we sat for a minute. The reverend was obviously in no hurry to let me go. I controlled the smile that wanted desperately to creep upon my face again.

I shifted in my seat and snored lightly. I heard that embarrassing sound and closed my eyes tighter. Reverend Baxter shook me gently.

"Christine," he whispered, "We're here. You're home."

I looked up at Revered Baxter through worn out eyes and smiled.

Reverend Baxter smiled back and rubbed my forehead.

"Wake up, sleepy head," he told me, "You're home."

I looked out of my window at Charles's car.

Suddenly, I felt ill. I could tell the reverend noticed the drastic change in my expression. His eyes told me he wanted so much to rescue me from whatever it was that was haunting me, and I wanted to let him, but that would mean exposing my ghost to him and I just wasn't ready for that.

I quickly thanked Reverend Baxter for the ride home. I wanted to invite him in, but I decided that might not be so wise a decision. I offered him my hand, my exposed five-chambered heart. He shook it. Neither of us let go. At that moment, our eyes met…and the tremor that I felt flooding in my soul let me know that our hearts did also.

—

Chapter 3 – Christine

"Why you going all over town looking for me?" Charles asked me with his forehead wrinkled and his fists clenched. "Showing everybody your eye. Were you really looking for me, or for pity? Do you know what you've done to me? Making me look like some kinda monster. You flattened my tires Christine, and you been a nag. All day every day, all you do is nag, nag, nag. Now you going around acting like I'm the bad one here. Making everybody think I beat on you. I hit you one time, just one time, and you gotta go around screaming that you're a battered wife?"

"I never said that, Charles," I told him. My legs were getting wobbly and my voice was quivering. For the first time, I realized, I'm afraid of Charles—very afraid.

"You might as well have," he retorted.

"Charles," I pleaded and stuttered in defending myself, "I covered my eye before I left home. I covered it real good too, but as I started to cry, I guess I forgot about the makeup washing off. I didn't mean you any harm. I just wanted to meet with you and to help you with your work the way I used to. That's all this was about, trying to get things back to the way they used to be."

"Things ain't never gonna be the same between us now. You got everybody watching me and probably filling your head with all kinds of garbage. I can't hold my head up high anymore. I can't go to the soup kitchen, to the hospital, on any of my missions anymore. Nobody wants me around. And church, well, I sure can't go there now, can I? You've ruined me. Totally disgraced me. I'm supposed to be at a Deacon Board meeting right now."

"You're not going?" I interrupted. In all the years Charles has been on the board, he has never missed a meeting.

"I ain't allowed to go, Christine. I ain't a board member no more. Reverend Baxter sent Deacon James to call me in to a meeting earlier today. I've been kicked off the board. Reverend Baxter said I am a total *mis-rep-re-sen-ta-tion*," he mocked, "of his teachings. He sat me down. That arrogant son of a..." Charles bit his bottom lip then continued. "In a church I've been going to all my life, I've been sat down. Christine, you just gone and done it this time."

I could see tears forming in my husband's eyes. He was hurt, far worse than any black eye and damaged feelings could have ever made me. This wound cut deep.

As Charles took his bags and jadedly headed upstairs, dragging one foot at a time, I felt a tightening in my chest. Things had gone so wrong today. Instead of drawing my husband nearer to me, I had succeeded in driving him even further away. I stood in the kitchen listlessly, not sure of what I should do next. I felt so weak and disoriented. I went into the living room and plopped my limp body down on the sofa. I stared up at the ceiling and watched the fan spin. My eyes got heavy, but I refused to give in. I wouldn't sleep my problems away today. That has always been my method of dealing with things in the past, but I couldn't let today's mishaps ruin my plan to get my marriage back on track. I had to think of a way to make things up to Charles.

Although Charles never accounted for how he actually had spent the day that seemed secondary now. I was more concerned with how to help Charles to redeem his character again. I went into the kitchen and found my purse. I dug my little address book out of it and searched for the number to the church. As much as I had dialed it before, I just couldn't remember the number right now. I dialed Reverend Baxter's office and prayed silently that he answered.

"Stone Hill Baptist Church, Reverend Conrad Baxter speaking. I looked up at the ceiling and mouthed a "Thank you," before answering.

"Reverend Baxter," I said, "It's me, Sister Rutherford," That sounded far more formal than I meant for it to. I quickly corrected myself. "It's…uh, Christine."

There was a slight pause.

"Christine. Are you alright?"

Reverend Baxter's voice was full of concern.

"I'm fine," I told him. "I just need to see you. I promise not to take up too much of your time."

"You can have all the time you need Christine, all the time you want."

My hands began to shake and my lower lip quivered. Suddenly, I had butterflies in my stomach.

"I'm leaving the house now, Reverend," I told him. "I should be at your office in about fifteen minutes."

"I'll be waiting," he answered.

I took a cup out of the cupboard and filled it with ice, and cold water. I felt warm and I needed to cool off. When I was done, I stood in the kitchen for a minute to compose myself.

"Charles," I yelled upstairs, "I have to go out for a minute. I'll be right back."

Charles didn't answer, but I was sure he had heard me. I took up my purse and keys and went out to my car. I looked at Charles's flattened tires. *I must remember to have those fixed*, I thought. But *right now, I've got something bigger to fix first*.

Before putting the key in the ignition, I remembered an important detail. I reached into my cosmetics bag for my compact and covered my eye. This time, I was sure to apply thick layers of foundation to the injured spot.

As I drove, I felt nervous and edgy. I decided to put on some soft music. That always manages to calm me down. I thumbed through my CD's and found the perfect song, CeCe Winans' *Alabaster Box*. I sang along with CeCe the entire way to the church.

I parked in the rear of the lot right next to Reverend Baxter's car. Just as I began to make my way out of the car, I spotted Reverend Baxter standing in the doorway, ready to greet me.

He smiled as I approached him. Then, he took my hand and led me to his office.

"Come on in, Christine. Did you manage to get much rest this afternoon?" he asked.

"No not really," I told him. The bags under my eyes were tell tale signs of that. "I guess I have too much on my mind. I really need to talk."

Reverend Baxter's smile turned into a look of apprehension. He could tell I had something heavy weighing on my heart. Once we reached his office, he motioned for me to have a seat. He shut the door.

"Would you prefer I leave the door ajar?" he asked.

Reverend Baxter always felt a little uncomfortable about having women in his office alone. He was often afraid of rumors starting and false allegations being made. He had fallen victim to one or two false allegations in the past, and since, he has exercised greater caution. I knew he felt safe with me though. For some reason, he's always expressed a need to shelter and protect me.

"No, this matter is private. It's already been publicized more than I'd like. I need to talk to you about Charles. I understand you've had him removed from the Deacon board."

Reverend Baxter watched me closely for a minute before answering. My hands were shaking and I was fidgeting in my chair. I hadn't made eye contact with him the entire time I spoke.

"Yes, Christine, I did have Charles removed from the Board. His character as of late is not representative of the way in which I expect my Deacons to behave. They are my agents and I am an agent of the Lord. Keeping Charles on the Board would mean, in an underlying sense, that I condone his behaviour and I do not," He put greater emphasis on the last two words.

I turned my face towards Reverend Baxter and made direct eye contact with him. I boldly stood and walked around to his side of the desk, invading his space the way he was invading my life.

"You can't judge Charles," I said furiously. "I never told you that Charles mistreated me. I never said that. You've come to your own conclusions and you have acted hastily based upon them. You have no right to treat my husband like he's some kind of criminal. Did you even hear him out before making your decision? Did you give him a chance to speak up and defend himself? Do you think you've done me a favour? Well, do you?"

My tears were falling all over Reverend Baxter's paperwork, smearing the ink.

"Christine, he hasn't hurt you any more, has he?" the Reverend asked.

"I never said that he hurt me. I never told you that," I retorted with my fists balled.

"But he did, Christine, didn't he?"

I didn't answer. Instead, I rose to leave. As I made my way towards the door, Reverend Baxter rushed to me and took me by the hand. He touched my chin gently and lifted it until my eyes met his.

"Talk to me, Chris. Let me help you. Don't cover it up, whatever it is, whatever's been done. Don't let him hurt you. Don't let anyone hurt you. Please, open up to me. I care about you. Don't you know that?" he told me. I could see he was being sincere.

I felt weak. I wanted to answer, but I didn't

know what to say. I felt the way I did when I was a little girl and my daddy would comfort me after I had injured myself in some way. I draped my arm around Reverend Baxter's neck and allowed my head to fall on his shoulders. I smelled the inviting scent of his cologne and closed my eyes.

Reverend Baxter put his arms around me and held me close. He laid his head on mine and stroked my hair. I looked up and the tip of my nose brushed against the Reverend's cheek. I shuddered. We held each other in a warm penetrating gaze.

Before I could control myself, I reached up and nibbled on the Reverend's quivering lower lip. I could tell by his slight hesitation that a part of him knew he should stop me, but a bigger part wouldn't let him. Instead, he put his hand behind my head, supporting my neck and he kissed me with intense passion for what seemed like an eternity. I felt a magnet drawing us together with force. I knew I should let go, but I just couldn't.

Once the kiss was over, I looked into the Reverend's guilt ridden eyes. I'm sure we both suddenly felt the way Adam and Eve must have when they discovered their nakedness.

Reverend Baxter and I had succumbed to lust. He turned his eyes from me and focused on the wall behind me where his plaque of the Ten Commandments lay. He raised his head towards Heaven and closed his eyes, but his hold on me remained strong. He was undoubtedly asking the Lord to forgive him for what he had done and to give him the strength he would need to refrain from what he yet desired to do.

Chapter 4 – Charles

"Aren't you going to work today, Charles?" Christine asked me. She had already showered and was taking her clothes out of the closet.

"Not feeling too good,"

I told her.

"You've been saying that for days. Don't you think you need to see a doctor? You're looking a little pale, Charles. I'd feel much better if you…" she started to babble.

I interrupted her, "I'm not feeling good and I'm not up for talking. Just leave me alone." Then, I rolled over and pulled the bed sheets up to my neck.

She took her dress off the bed and hung it back in the closet.

"Want something to eat. Toast or something? Is your stomach aching again?"

I looked at her. For the past couple of days, she had been tending to me like a mother hen. I was suspicious as to why.

I could tell that my examining her was making her uncomfortable. She began pacing around the room, straightening things that were already straight and hand dusting furniture that had already been dusted.

"I don't want nothing but some peace," I told her.

She turned and headed down the stairs to the living room. She went to the bookshelf and grabbed the souvenir bell from a trip we had taken to Florida. She came back upstairs and placed the bell on the nightstand closest to me.

"Here," she told me, "Ring if you need anything. I'll be downstairs."

I looked her dead in the eyes, letting my suspicions be known. She turned away.

"Humph," I grunted before rolling completely over on my side. I listened for her to make her way down the stairs. Once I knew she was out of earshot, I picked up the phone.

"Dr. Kaylor's office," replied the raspy voice on the other end.

"This is Charles Rutherford. I need to see Dr. Kaylor today," I told her.

"Dr. Kaylor is only in until noon today, sir, and she's already booked. She only opens one Saturday out of every month and she's always booked by seven a.m. If you have a medical emergency, I suggest you call the hospital. If not, I'll be happy to make an appointment for you for some time next week."

I didn't answer. I hung up the phone, and then I sat on the bed and held my stomach. The pain I was feeling was unbearable. I took a deep breath and let out a light moan. The last thing I wanted was for Christine to hear.

I closed my eyes and said a silent prayer. Within minutes, I was able to rise to my feet and make my way to my dresser drawer. I took out a pair of charcoal grey sweats and white socks. I dressed myself slowly while trying to wrestle with the pain. Once I was completely dressed, I took up my coat and hat and started down the stairs. Christine was on her way up. The two of us stopped mid way, each surprised to see the other.

"Charles, you're up," Christine said, "and dressed."

"I got somewhere I need to be." I told her with my head down.

"But I thought you weren't feeling well. I was just coming up to…"

I cut her off. "I told you that you didn't need to stay at home with me. I don't need no babysitter Christine."

Christine's eyes watered. "I'm your wife, Charles." She started, "It's my duty to take care of you. I wish you would let me. I wish you would stop treating me like I'm less than human."

Her voice got louder and her tears fell faster.

"I wish you would talk to me. I wish you would let me hold you. I wish you would let me love you. I wish you would just find it somewhere inside to love me. And you know what I wish most Charles? I wish that you would just let me go if you can't do those things. Why do you stay here if you're so unhappy? Why do you treat me the way you do? I don't deserve it. Do you hear what I'm saying to you, Charles? I don't deserve this. God knows I don't. All I ever do is try to please you, to stay out of your way since that seems to make you most happy these day, but we're married, Charles. You are my husband, and I am your wife, and you vowed before God to love me till death parts us. Have you met with the grim reaper, Charles? Have you?"

Without giving me a chance to say anything, Christine ran up the stairs and slammed the bedroom door shut. I could hear her crying. I walked up the stairs and stood outside the door for a minute, listening to the whimpering sounds my wife was making. I tapped gently on the door.

"Christine," I called out.

"Chris…?"

Christine didn't answer. I decided to give her a bit of time to herself. Besides, I had no idea how to make things right when everything between us was going so wrong. I felt a tear run down my cheek. I quickly wiped it away with my shirtsleeve and started down the stairs. I found my car keys on the kitchen counter, right next to my and Christine's wedding album. Christine must have taken it from its resting place in the box in the cabinet below our entertainment unit and been looking through it. It was open to a picture of the two of us locked in an embrace at our wedding reception. It was plain to see that we were in love. Another tear fell from my eye.

I suddenly felt a gripping pain in my stomach. I held onto it and stumbled my way to my car.

Dr. Kaylor would see me today. She has to. The pain I'm feeling is becoming unbearable and upsetting Christine is hurting me more that she could know, but I just can't tell her the truth. She would worry and become overly protective. I don't need that. The last thing I need is her pity.

When I look at her, I see a soft, tenderhearted, dedicated Christian wife who is gradually becoming more independent, more vengeful, more cunning, and more self-preserving than she has ever been. Without completely ruining who she used to be, I need her to develop into the type of person she will soon need to be. I can't leave her until I know that she will be able to handle herself. She's been sheltered nearly all her life, first by her father, and then by me. She's never lived alone, had to make major decisions, or seen her name at the top of a bill. If she had to pay one, she wouldn't know how to write a cheque or where to go to buy a stamp. It might seem cruel, but my indifference to Chrissy is grooming her for what's to come. She asked me if I've met with the grim reaper. I haven't yet, but I know his chariot will be pulling up in my driveway real soon.

I'm halfway down Fifth and Main when I consider taking the longer route to Dr. Kaylor's office so that I can avoid passing by the church. I feel uncomfortable going anywhere near there now that I have been exposed to and banned from the Deacon Board.

At first, I was mad as hell at Reverend Baxter for taking actions against me. I felt like that sanctimonious man suddenly thought he was God himself. It only took a day for me to cool off and to reflect. Now that I have managed to step back and take a full look at things, I feel ashamed of myself and undeserving of not only going into the house of the Lord, but going anywhere within a five-mile radius of it also.

Christine, on the other hand, has been going there quite often. She has been seeking the Reverend's counsel a whole lot lately. In one sense, I'm glad she's talking through her pain, but I wish she didn't feel the need to tell everything that's been going on between us.

I feel the pain in my stomach defeating me again. I need to see Dr. Kaylor. She needs to provide me with some type of relief from the suffering I've been enduring. She needs to give me something to ease my body and my spirit.

Maybe it's time I made things up to Chris. Maybe I've groomed her for Hell long enough. She needs a pain reliever too. Tonight, I'll let Chris know that I'm sick. I won't tell her everything, but I will tell her enough to make her aware that my behaviour is beyond my total control. I'll hold her when I tell her. I'll make her feel like my wife again. I'll give in and let her see my vulnerability. I'm tired of fighting this never-ending battle. Maybe it's time I surrender, but before I give in completely, I've got amends to make and preparations to put in place. I've got to give Christine all the things I promised God I would, and most of all, I'll give her what she's been wanting for years now, a living, breathing blend of the two of us. I'll leave a part of me behind.

As I turn into the parking lot of Dr. Kaylor's office, I shut off the car engine and wipe the tears that are flowing down my cheeks. I recline my seat, hold my stomach, and pray. "God," I say, "From here, it's all up to you. No more interference from me. Make it clear to me what I need to do to make things right for Christine. Help me to prepare Chris and myself for what is soon to come. I hear you calling me. I hear you telling me my hourglass is almost empty. That my room is being prepared. Give me the last bit of strength I will need to…" I clutch my stomach and sit upright. I've got to make it inside. I've got to start preparing for my end.

Chapter 5 - Christine

I heard Charles's car pull out of the driveway. I tried to pick myself up from the tear soaked spot where I lay, but my limp body fought any movement. I felt a throbbing pain in my head like never before. After moments of suffering, I picked myself up and went into the medicine cabinet in search of Tylenol. I found the bottle on the top shelf, but to my surprise, it was empty. I was sure that it was the same bottle I had purchased only a couple of weeks ago. I fumbled around the cabinet for something else that would help to take the pain away. I didn't find anything in the cabinet, but I knew where I could find some relief. I would seek out Reverend Baxter. He has become my doctor, and his addictive kiss has become my cure all. I was ready for him to heal me once and for all.

I packed my belongings and guiltlessly headed out in search of the reverend. He would be easy to find. Unlike Charles, Reverend Baxter was easily accessible and always happy to see me. As I drove, I felt a spirit of rebelliousness taking over. I knew I needed to pray for serenity, but I couldn't just now. I wanted to feel rebellious. I was tired of being the good wife, the passive party, the doormat.

I wound the window down in my car and allowed the wind to dry my tears. I made a silent resolution to stop crying over Charles and to start caring more for myself. I would take charge of my emotions from now on. I was determined that the tears I had shed today would be my last.

The traffic was heavy and I was impatient. I sped my way down the main strip. As I whizzed in and out of traffic, car horns blew, drivers cussed, and red lights proved not to be my friend, but I stepped heavily on the gas and continued on my way, a woman on a mission. It usually took fifteen to twenty minutes to make it to the church, but I managed to arrive there in less than ten.

I looked around the empty lot for Reverend Baxter's car. I searched the front of the church. The only car on the lot was an abandoned one that had been resting there for weeks. I drove around to the back near the Reverend's office where I was sure he must have been parked. The Reverend's car wasn't there either. I sat in the vacant lot and hung my head and cried. I laid my head on the steering wheel and let my tears fall. Within a matter of moments, I wiped my eyes and repositioned myself in my seat. I felt that spirit of rebelliousness creeping up on me again. I started the engine and roared my way on to the busy highway. I drove seventeen miles before arriving at my destination. I carefully read the street signs. I found the one I was looking for, Bennington Lane.

I drove over a small hill and arrived at a gorgeous three-story brick home with beautiful landscaping. I saw a light on in what must have been the living room area. A figure walked towards the window and looked out. I shut off my engine and sat for a minute.

The figure appeared at the entrance of the home and peered at me. It was a woman, approximately twenty years old, and very beautiful. Suddenly, I felt awkward and ready to run.

"Can I help you," yelled the person at the door.

Reverend Baxter came to the door and stood behind her. He put his hand on the woman's shoulder and glanced over her head. He gently moved her to the side and stepped outdoors. He moved closer to the car. I sat there unable to move a muscle. My body shook and my lips started to quiver. As the Reverend approached the driver's side of the car, the pounding of my heart became so prominent that I was sure he would be able to hear it beating.

"Christine?" he said as he looked at me through the windowpane.

I hesitated for a moment then rolled down my window.

"Hi. I went to your office, but you weren't there and I just wanted to…I just thought I would" I mumbled like a stuttering fool.

Reverend Baxter could see tension all over my face.

"Are you alright, Christine? Is there something you would like for me to do for you?" he asked me in a sympathetic tone.

I looked at the entrance of Reverend Baxter's home at the woman who was still standing in the doorway.

"No," I replied. "I shouldn't've come. It can wait."
"You're welcome to come inside," he told me.

"No," I quickly answered, "Thank you."

At that moment, tears fell. I tried to hide my face, but Reverend Baxter had already witnessed my distress. He opened the car door and reached for my hand.

"Come inside, Christine.
Please," he begged.

I placed my hand in his and followed the reverend. On the way, I was sure I would stumble and fall. My legs were wobbly and I thought they would give out on me.

Reverend Baxter, noticing how unsteady I was, put his arm around my waist to provide greater balance. I loved the way his manly arm secured me. I thought of how I would hate it once he would let go.

"Yes," he answered her, "Bring Christine a cup also, won't you, Sweetie?"

Sweetie? I thought. My plastered grin slowly faded.

Stacey nodded and quickly left the room, eager to please. I fumbled with my fingers some more.

"You have a beautiful home," I told the reverend. "Nice pictures."

"Thank you, but my wife deserves all the credit. She took pride in our quarters. This was all her doing," he modestly answered.

Great, I thought, *I've made him think of his wife while the present woman in his life fixes my tea.*

"She did a fantastic job," I managed to say through gritted teeth.

Just then, Stacey reemerged carrying a tray

of tea and shortbread cookies.

"Thought you'd like some cookies too," she told the reverend. "You sure do know how to take care of me," he responded.

"That's why I keep you around. Besides that, you're far cheaper than a maid." He chuckled and Stacey laughed and playfully smacked him on the head.

I sipped my tea and pretended not to notice.

"You keep me around because you love me and you know it. You don't know what to do with yourself without me," Stacey teased as she placed her hand on the reverend's shoulder.

"I sure do. I sure do," he responded as he reached up and held onto her hand.

"You gonna have some tea with us?" he asked Stacey.

"Nah, she told him. I'm gonna be late for work if I don't get out of here soon. I'm working a double shift, so don't wait up for me tonight."

I felt my blood boiling. I wanted to kick, scream, and cry, but instead, I shoved a cookie in my mouth and tried to occupy myself by glancing at the pictures again. This time, I noticed one of Stacey and the reverend. They were at a picnic of some sort. Stacey was wearing shorts and a cropped tee and had a towel draped around her neck. The reverend had on jeans and a polo shirt. He was laughing and raising a can of coke to the camera - man. They appeared to be having a great time together.

I suddenly felt the need to be alone. I felt foolish and invasive. I stood to tell the reverend that I had to be leaving, but as I did, Stacey walked over to me, offered her hand again, and told me how delighted she was that we had met. I shook her hand and grimaced.

"I'm glad I had the opportunity to meet you as well," I told her. "You're definitely one of Reverend Baxter's best kept secrets." Those words came out far more scornfully than I intended.

Reverend Baxter raised a brow then smiled. Stacey raised her brow as well.

"Well, I'd better get going. You two enjoy your tea party," Stacey told us.

"I'll see you later, Revvy," Stacey told the reverend. "Don't forget that I won't be home until late. Remember to leave the outside light on for me, okay?" She kissed his cheek.

With that, she waved at both the reverend and me, and bounced her way out of the living room.

"I've got to be going too," I said irritably. I couldn't hide my emotions any longer. "I never should've come. I apologize for intruding. I'm...I..." Tears muted the words I tried to say.

Reverend Baxter offered me a napkin off the tray. I wiped my eyes and sniffled loudly.

"Christine, what's the matter? You haven't been yourself since you got here. Please don't go without telling me the problem. I'm here for you," he told me.

"Aren't your hands full enough?" I snapped. "I came here because I needed to talk. More than that, I needed a friend. Charles has become so distant. More so than before, and being in the house with him is driving me crazy. I needed someone to talk to who I knew would listen and would be there for me. I needed…Oh, never mind. I shouldn't have come. I'm sorry. Please forgive me. I need to learn how to handle my own affairs."

"Christine, you are a member of my congregation. It's my duty to help you. That's what I'm there for, to help those in need and to inspire the uninspired. To help souls that are lost. To provide hope to those who feel that their situations are hopeless," He told me.

"Don't preach to me, Reverend. I don't need you to service me, to fulfill a duty or an obligation. I need a friend. I didn't come here to hire you to perform any task for me. I came because…I don't know why I came."

"Christine, I didn't mean it like that. I am your friend. Go ahead, lean on me," the reverend pleaded.

"Which shoulder should I lean on?" I asked scathingly. "I don't want to invade Stacey's space."

I turned away, ashamed and angry with myself for letting my jealousy show. The reverend placed both of his hands on my shoulders and gently spun me around to face him.

"Christine," he smiled flatteringly, "Stacey is my niece. Forgive me for not including that information in your introduction. I wasn't thinking."

I hung my head. I was terribly ashamed now.

"Your niece?" I echoed to be sure I had heard him correctly. "Stacey is your niece?"

"Yes," he grinned. "She's my wife's niece actually. She's full of life and character. She's one of my favourites. I spoil her, as I am sure you can tell. She comes by to keep me company while she's on breaks from school. Stacey attends Penn State. She's studying to be a nurse. She's doing part of her internship while she's here. She'll be here for another three weeks. I'm curious, who did you think she was?

I sat on the sofa. My legs couldn't hold me up anymore. I hung my head and covered my face with my hands. I was relieved, but extremely ashamed.

Reverend Baxter sat beside me.

"Christine," he giggled, "Did you think Stacey was some woman I've been seeing? Someone I've been having an affair with?"

My facial expression must have confirmed his theory. He laughed out loud and slapped his knee.

"I'm sorry, Christine, I really am. I don't mean to make you feel worse than you already do, but that's hilarious. I'm flattered to know you think I've got it in me to attract a beautiful young woman like Stacey."

"Why wouldn't I think that?" I asked. "You've certainly attracted me."

The laughter stopped. The room was still. The reverend could see that I was serious. He penetrated me with his eyes. I felt a rush of anxiety come over me, and I did what came naturally. I placed my hand on the reverend's knee and moved in close to him. It was *his* body that was quivering now.

I reached up and touched his cheek. The revered remained still and hypnotized by the bold new woman before him. My hand moved behind the reverend's neck. I locked it in place and slowly pulled his head forward. I went out on a limb and placed my warm, ready lips against his. The kiss started off softly and quickly became passionate and expressive.

—

Almost twenty-five minutes passed before either of us felt the least bit guilty. Neither of us wanted to let the other go or to rejoin our lonely and loveless worlds. We wished we could remain together forever, and we told each other so. I told the reverend of how I wished I were no longer married to Charles, and he confessed to me that he wished the same.

Chapter 6 - Christine

"Mr. Rutherford, I explained to you on the phone that Dr. Kaylor wouldn't be taking any more patients today," said the condescending, stubby, middle aged Minnie Pearl look alike receptionist.

"And I told you I needed to see her today," was my reply. "I'm not leaving until I do. Tell her Charles Rutherford is here..." I asserted myself and stated my name like I was the president of the United States. I looked at the name on the desk plaque before me, "Mildred," I sarcastically added.

Mildred's entire face turned a blush red shade. She rolled her eyes, spun herself around in her swivel chair, which squeaked in pain, and stood slowly.

"I'll let her know you're here *Charles*," she mocked, "but I can't promise she'll see you, and if she says she can't you'll just have to go. Like I told you earlier, I'm willing to make other arrangements for you." She waited for my answer. I just smiled at her, turned and found an empty seat. I nodded my head towards the door to Dr. Kaylor's office. Mildred turned and found an empty seat. I nodded my head towards the door to Dr. Kaylor's office. Mildred sucked her teeth, knocked once on the door, and then let herself in.

She returned less than two minutes later. Her face now looked like a turnip.

"She'll see you when she's done seeing everybody else that has appointments. I don't know how long that'll be. It could be a while yet," she informed me.

"Thank you, Millie," I teased with a victorious grin, "I can wait."

I picked up a magazine and started thumbing through it. Inside were pictures of families, the kind Christine and I never started. I saw children holding their daddy's hands, mother's at playgrounds chatting with other mothers, grandparents playing with their grandkids in the yard. I began to image Christine and I sharing that kind of joy. I fought back tears that were determined to flow. I put the magazine back in its place. I looked up. Millie was staring at me. Her face was softer now and a lovely shade of soft pink. She smiled a sympathetic smile before continuing with her paperwork. I looked at each of the other patients in the office, two older gentlemen and a young woman, and tried to imagine why they were here. I tried to figure out if their lives were in as bad a shape as mine. It's sad but true. Misery does like company.

Dr. Kaylor stepped out of her office right behind her patient, a young blonde woman. She reached for her chart and read off the next name on the list, Connie Lemmons. As she looked around at those of us who were left, she made eye contact with me and gave a wink. She has a way of making her patients feel like she really cares. I'm glad Christine found her for us. The Yellow Pages are worth something after all.

I sat in the office for what felt like an eternity. The pains in my stomach fluctuated in intensity. Each time I clutched my aching belly, Millie would nervously glance up at me. Once I was finally the last patient waiting, Millie grunted out,

"You want some water or something?"

"No thanks, I told her. I don't think water will fix this one."

"Doc should be through with Miss Lemmons in a minute. She ain't here for nothing serious," she told me.

I just nodded my head and got as comfortable as I could. I laid my head back and closed my eyes. The room was quiet and still. It was nice. I thought pleasant thoughts of when I was younger. I remembered some of my happier moments and smiled. My thoughts were soon interrupted by a bubbly voice.

"Whew, am I late? I'm not late am I? Goodness gracious, the traffic coming along Mercer was a beast. Has Doc been looking for me?" she asked.

I opened my eyes and saw a young, beautiful, black girl. She looked at me and said to Millie, "Only one patient, huh? Been slow today?"

Millie scowled at her. "That's Mr. Rutherford," she informed her. "He's our last patient of the day. Doctor Kaylor wants to take you over to the hospital later on and introduce you to some of the staff there. I think you'll help her to check on some of her patients."

"Oh, cool. That'll be good." She replied. She then turned her attention over to me. "Mr. Rutherford, huh? Rutherford must be a pretty popular name around here. I just met a lady named Rutherford about half hour ago. She was visiting with my Uncle Conrad."

I grimaced. "You just met another Rutherford? What was her name?"

"I think it was Christine. Yeah, Christine, that's it. You know her?" she innocently asked me.

I felt a tightening in my stomach. I couldn't believe what I was hearing, but I had to be sure not to blow my cover. I suddenly felt the need to further investigate. I didn't like the thoughts that were crashing through my mind. I needed this young woman to clarify the details for me.

"No, I don't know her," I lied. "Where'd you say you met her?"

"She was at my Uncle Conrad's. I'm staying with my Uncle while I'm here visiting from Penn State. I'm doing my internship. I guess I get the pleasure of working with you today. You'll be my guinea of the day," she giggled.

"You're staying with your Uncle Conrad, huh? Is he a pretty popular guy?" I tried not to sound suspicious.

"Yeah, I guess you could say so," she said. "He's the Pastor of a church just off of Fifth and Main."

My stomach was wrenching now, and my head was pounding. I felt warm, and beads of sweat started to roll off my face.

"You alright?" the young woman asked me. "You really are sick, aren't you? You want me to get something, do something for you?"

"Leaving him alone for a little while until the doctor is ready to see him might be a good idea," Millie snarled.

"Sorry, sir, I didn't know that all my babbling would get you so worked up. Go ahead and rest until Doctor Kaylor calls for you," she said softly and apologetically.

I didn't respond. I was still trying to digest the fact that the young woman had informed me that she had seen my wife only moments ago at the home of Conrad Baxter. It was all making sense to me now. Christine's pleasantries, and her attentiveness, my being so quickly dismissed from the Deacon Board, Christine's frequent trips to the church. I started to cry. Like a baby, I sat there with tears coming down my cheeks. It was hard to notice my tears from the sweat pouring down my face. I quickly snatched a tissue from Millie's tissue box and wiped my head and my eyes before she could see my vulnerability.

"I don't need to see the doctor after all," I told Mildred. "I just need a little rest. I'm tired. Pencil me in for next week, won't you?"

Before Mildred could answer, Doctor Kaylor emerged from her office.

"Oh, Stacey," she said to the young woman. "You made it, huh? Wash your hands and meet me in the back room. Mr. Rutherford, it's finally your turn. Come on in."

I left my belongings right there in the waiting room and went into Dr. Kaylor's office. I felt light-headed and disoriented.

"You're not looking too good, Charles. What's

been going on?" she asked me. She pulled out a chair and motioned, "Here, sit down. Talk to me."

Still thinking about the possibility of Christine and Conrad Baxter, I cried some more. Doctor Kaylor mistook my tears for a sign of unbearable pain. She helped me up from the chair and led me to her back room. She helped me to get positioned onto the bed and began checking my pulse. She frowned. She proceeded to check my temperature, my heart rate, etc. As she worked on me, I worked on fighting stubborn tears. She raised my shirt and felt my stomach. She pressed on different sections of it and I made an ugly face each time. She sent me to pee in a cup. When I was done, she asked me a series of questions. By that time, the young black woman appeared and immediately started taking notes. Doctor Kaylor remained focused on me.

"Have you been taking your pills, Charles?" She asked. "Sometimes." I answered indifferently.

"Charles, your condition is serious. I'm not going to sugar coat this for you. You need to take your pills if you have any desire to prolong your life. Do you realize what you're up against? Don't you care about what's at stake? Don't you want to live?"

I gave Doctor Kaylor a look that suggested I didn't.

"What's going on, Charles?" she asked. "You want to talk about it? How can I help you if you won't help yourself?"

"What?" the young woman answered.

"You heard me," I told her. "I'm not asking. You're working here, and your seeing me and telling it would violate some type of patient client confidentiality clause, wouldn't it?"

"I guess so," she said.

"Well, there you have it then. You're not allowed legally or morally to tell her you met me. That's our secret. Don't ever mention me to Christine. Promise me you won't. Don't mention me to your uncle either."

"I won't," she said softly. "I promise."

She sat and stared at me for a moment. I could tell she had something on her mind.

"Whatsa matter with you?" I asked her.

"What's the matter with you?" she mirrored back.

"I've got a bad case of Mesothelioma. You know what that is? You come to that part of your course work yet?"

"No," she said sullenly.

"What's that?"

"It's a type of stomach cancer," I told her.

"It's a very bad type of stomach cancer," Dr. Kaylor said as she came back into the room. "Especially if you don't take care of it and keep in touch with your doctor." She was looking punitively at me. "You're going to the hospital. I'm checking you in."

I opened my mouth to interrupt her, but she saw that quickly and she wouldn't let me.

"Don't argue with me. What happens to you from now on is not up to you. You are my patient, and I am not going to lose you without a fight. I won't sit back and watch you just give up. You've got no choice in the matter, Charles. You're going in and you'll stay as long as it's necessary. Do you need me to call and explain all of this to Christine, or will you be a good boy and handle this yourself?

—

I looked at my new confidant as I answered, "I'll take care of Christine. Don't you worry yourself about that."

"Good," she said. "Here's the plan. You've got one hour to go home, pack any toiletries and other necessities; things that will make you feel more comfortable during your stay. You will meet me in the lobby of Grand Valley Memorial in exactly one hour and fifteen minutes. Don't be late and don't make me come looking for you. How are you feeling?"

"A little nervous," I told her.

"Physically, I mean," she said. "How are you feeling physically right now?"

"I'll be alright."

I turned to leave. My feet suddenly felt heavy, but they finally made it to the door.

"One hour and fifteen minutes, Charles," Doctor Kaylor said.

I waved my hand to let her know I had heard. I gathered my things in the waiting room and thought about how I would get away with gathering my things at home.

Chapter 7 – Christine

When I got home, the house was in darkness and Charles was nowhere to be found. I was concerned because he never stayed out past dark. I checked the phone for a message from him, but during the time we were out, we'd only received one call and it was from Ellen Bradshaw. She had called earlier to ask if I would be willing to make some brownies for the bake sale being hosted by the Children's Church. I knew the call was a mere follow up, so I decided to make a mental note to call her back a little later.

I was tired. I hurried to my bedroom where I could get in a quick nap while Charles was still out. I plunked myself down on the bed and heard a crunching noise under me. I sat up and spotted a sheet of notebook paper. I turned on the lamplight so I could make out what was written on it.

I put my hand over my mouth and let out a wail. I put the paper down on the bed and quickly checked Charles's chest of drawers. They weren't completely empty, but it was obvious that most of his socks and underwear were missing. I went to the bathroom. His toothbrush, shaving cream, and headache pills were also gone. I looked in the closet. Some items of his clothing were missing from there too. Charles had left me. He had finally packed up and left me. I went back to the bed and read the note again.

Christine,

> *I won't be home tonight. As a matter of fact, I won't be home for quite a few nights. I'm not exactly sure how long I'll be gone, but I don't want you to worry about me. I've left you some money on the kitchen counter in the old cookie canister. I've left my credit card there too in case you find you'll need some more. There's something I have to tell you. Something I should have told you a long time ago. Things will be clearer when I see you again. I promise we'll have a good talk. I want you to know that I'm sorry for all that's happened between us. I never meant for things to go so wrong. I hope that one day, you'll find it in your heart to forgive me. I do love you, Christine, but there's not much more I can do for you now. Live your life. Be happy. Pay no regards to me. It's time for you to do for yourself whatever it is your heart tells you to do. I love you. I've always loved you, but sometimes, life throws us curve balls that mess up everything we intend to accomplish. Those curve balls have drastically changed my life. Let them change yours too, for the better.*

> *Charles*

I crumpled the note and threw it to the floor. I put my head in my hands and shamelessly cried out loud. My husband had left me. Without a clue as to where he had gone or how I could reach him, he left. I felt lost, empty, and very much unloved. The seriousness of the state of my marriage had just slapped me in the face. I thought about all the things that must have gone wrong between us and blamed myself for all of them. I thought of how I probably could have saved my marriage if I weren't so inhibited, so homely, so uninteresting, so nagging.

I should have asserted myself more, grabbed my man by the reins tighter, taken greater control of our marriage, not been such a doormat. Maybe Charles saw me as weak. All kinds of thoughts ran through my mind.

I turned the lamp light out, sat in the dark, and cried for hours. The more I tried to sort everything out in my mind, the more confused I became. My marriage was ending and from the sounds of Charles's note and the fact that he's just up and gone, there's nothing I can do about it.

I must have cried myself to sleep. An hour and ten minutes had passed. My head was throbbing and I felt dizzy. I needed something to help to relieve the pain. I got up and made my way to the bathroom. The medicine cabinet didn't contain much. I headed downstairs to make sure all the doors were securely locked and to make myself a cup of hot tea. I filled the kettle, put the water on, and reached for the box of Sleepy Time. I needed a tranquilizer. Usually, I used Calme Forte pills, but tonight, a hot cup of tea would have to do.

I had only managed to take one sip when the phone rang. I checked the caller ID. The call had been blocked.

"Hello," I answered lethargically.

"Christine?" questioned the voice on the other end. "Charles? Is that you?" I asked as tears fell. "Yeah, it's me," he said.

"Where are you? Why did you leave? When will you be back? Can't we talk about this? How could you just leave me? Write me a cryptic note and just leave? How could you do that?" I said all of that in virtually one breath, not giving him a chance to answer.

"I know you must be upset, Chris. I know you've got tons of questions, but all I can tell you is that I am where I need to be right now. I'm…. I'm…. I'm being taken care of," he told me.

By this time, I was fed up. I didn't want to play his game.

"Yeah, Charles, I'm sure you are being taken care of. You know, Charles, I just spent the past couple of hours crying over you, but not anymore. I'm all cried out. I'm glad you're being taken care of. Don't worry about me. I'll be taken care of too." I hung up and I slammed the phone down over and over again. I felt such rage. I beat up on the phone the way I wanted to beat up on Charles.

I didn't know what Charles was trying to prove, but what I did know was that it was time for me to start taking charge of my life. I felt a surge of energy all of a sudden. I threw my tea down the sink. No more crutches.

I went around the house and collected everything that had Charles' name or his fingerprints on it; clothes he left behind, cologne bottles, shoes, books, pictures, you name it. I shabbily stacked all of his belongings in the middle of the living room floor. Then, I went to the basement and retrieved some of the large empty boxes we'd been saving for no good reason at all. I threw all of his belongings into those boxes. Normally I would fold, label, and categorize, but not tonight. I sealed the boxes, which to me symbolized also sealing my fate. No longer would I suffer abuse and neglect like a stray puppy. Charles' game was official over. It's time to play a new game by my rules.

I stacked the boxes one on top of the other and placed them in the corner of the living room where they would be easily accessible whenever Charles decided to return. Tomorrow, I'll change the locks.

I looked around the living room as I thought about what else a woman in my position might do. I couldn't think of anything but celebrating my newfound freedom. I hurried upstairs and ran a bath. I loaded the tub with bubbles and lit a candle. I turned off the bathroom light and let the warm water hug my body.

As I lay there, taking in the scent of gardenias, tears started to fall again. I quickly wiped them away. I refuse to let any more tears fall. I started to softly sing the first verse and the chorus of *His Eye Is On The Sparrow*,

> *"Why should I feel discouraged?*
> *And why should the shadows come*
> *Why should my heart be lonely*
> *And long for Heav'n and home,*

When Jesus is my portion, My constant
Friend is He; His eye is on the sparrow,
And I know He watches over me.
I sing because I'm happy,
I sing because I'm free;
For His eye is on the sparrow,
And I know He watches over me.

The warm water made me think of other things that warmed me, my friend Sandi in North Carolina who I haven't spoken to in months. I'll give her a call tomorrow. With thanks to Charles, I'll also buy myself some new clothes and some fresh makeup. Ruby red lipstick will top my list. I'll go to Barbara's Bump A Curl too. My do could stand to be done. Charles hates short hairstyles for women and thinks adding colour is scandalous. Humph! I wonder if honey blonde accents would compliment my skin tone.

As I thought more and more about Charles, my head started to pound and as I sank deeper into despair, I submerged my body more and more into the water. A part of me wanted to bury my head beneath the surface and drown. Another part told me I should be glad Charles was gone, and flashed pictures in my mind of how life could be for me from now on. I saw myself venturing out more, socializing again, smiling, and walking proudly, with a child holding my left hand while Reverend Baxter firmly held my right. I hadn't thought about it until now, but the thought of a future with Reverend Baxter made me smile. When God closes one door, he truly does open another.

I pulled the plug in the bathtub and released my wet security blanket. I won't need it anymore tonight. I reached for a towel and noticed myself for the first time in the nearly full-length mirror. My nakedness was lovely. I stood there for a minute, and admired myself, the new me: bold, free, uninhibited, and beautiful. I smiled at what I saw and felt pity because of the true picture of me Charles couldn't see.

Chapter 8 – Charles

I must have called Christine over a dozen times last night. She refused to answer any more of my calls. I hope she is able to manage with out me. I know that she harbors a hidden strength deep within her, but I hope she is aware of that also. I hate that I had to leave her without warning, without preparation of any kind, but none of what's been going on lately has been up to me.

I'm at the mercy of doctors, nurses, and those darned outreach ministers who have already visited me twice, witnessing, and giving me one last chance to save my soul. I told them the first time around that they were preaching to the converted. Their second visit lets me know they didn't believe me.

I've been up since the crack of dawn being poked, and having my pressure and temperature taken every couple of minutes. Between my heavy head and my burdened spirit, I need a minute to close my eyes and escape it all.

Just as I turn over to drift off to sleep, I hear the squeaking of my door opening. I shut my eyes

Just as I turn over to drift off to sleep, I hear the squeaking of my door opening. I shut my eyes quickly to pretend I'm already asleep. I can't be bothered with seeing another figure in white riding in on a needle or a thermometer with the intention of saving me from the death angel.

"Charles," the person whispered.

I didn't answer.

"Charles," she said again. "Are you asleep?"

I always thought that was a stupid question.

Again, I respond by not responding.

I heard a chair squeaking. She must have sat down. I waited another couple of seconds. There was silence in the room. Minutes went by. I listened intently for the person to leave my room. She didn't. I was curious now as to who had invaded my space.

I shifted slightly, trying to peek peripherally at who was seated in the chair beside me. I saw part of a body, but no face. I angled my body more to the right to see the person head on.

"Hi. Did I wake you?" she said.

It was Stacey. She was dressed in a pretty sheer pink top, wide legged blue jeans and she had a pink and blue African styled head wrap covering her straight black hair. She was wearing a bit of makeup in subtle shades, which was beautifully applied, not overdone. She looked a lot older than she did when I met her yesterday.

"Hey," I said.

"Did I wake you?" she asked me again.

"Nah. I was just resting my eyes." I told her. "They don't let me sleep around here."

"I won't stay long. I hope you don't mind

that I've come. I know you need your rest, but I just wanted to make sure you were doing all right and that you didn't need anything. Have you called your wife yet, told her where you are? She coming to see you?"

I smiled, grateful for her concern.

"First, you can stay as long as you like. I could actually use some good company."

She lowered her head and smiled.

"And in answer to the rest of your questions, yes, I have called Christine. I called her last night. No, I didn't tell her where I am, and therefore, no, she won't be coming to see me." I told her.

That led to more questions. A series of them.

"Why didn't you tell her where you are? *Where* did you tell her you are? She must be worried about you. I don't understand you at all. Don't you want to see your wife? Don't you think you should tell her you're…that you're…?"

She stopped. I guess she just couldn't work her mouth to say the word *dying*, like she thought somehow saying it would make me keel over on the spot and she'd have to be the one to pick me up off the floor.

"I didn't tell her where I am," I started to explain, "because she doesn't even know that I'm sick. Telling her over the phone that I've been hospitalized, and that I'll probably die soon is not listed in the book of etiquette, now is it?" I smiled. She didn't.

"It's nice to see you have a sense of humour still," she said sullenly.

"That's all I've got to hold onto, and I ain't even got much of that left, if the truth be known," I told her. "To be honest with you, Stacey, there's a lot that's worrying me right now, but I'm trying not to let the worrying be the thing that kills me. Hell, this Mesothelioma I got is doing alright all by itself."

"Doc says you ain't got a whole lot longer. Couple of months max. Don't you think your wife would like to spend those last couple of months by your side? Don't you want to be by hers?" she asked me.

"Life ain't that easy. It's far more complicated than it appears. You'll learn that as you get a little older and go through a little more."

I could tell she didn't like my implying she was a little girl who hadn't gone through much. Her sad eyes told me she just might have.

"I'm real grateful for your concern," I told her, "but tell me, why are you so interested in what Christine or I might want? We're strangers to you. Young girl like you shouldn't be spending her time worrying about a dying man and his cheating wife."

"Allegedly cheating wife," she corrected me. Then she stood and picked up her purse. "You're right," she said with tears in her eyes, "I don't know why I'm so interested. Something just sent me this way. Something sent me here to check on you. Something's burning inside of me to take care of you. Something's...Oh never mind. I'm sorry I disturbed you."

At that very moment, she reminded me of Christine. I felt just as badly as I had when I met Christine on the stairs and sent her running to our bedroom. I have a knack for hurting people. That was becoming more and more clear. I couldn't comfort Christine then, but I could comfort Stacey now.

"Sit down, Stacey. Please. Don't go. I'm sorry. Please stay." I asked her.

She hesitated for a moment and glared at me, but she eventually sat. I reached for her hand.

"This..." I had trouble finding the right word. "...*situation* has me all messed up. One minute I'm alright and can deal with it fine, the next, I'm angry and confused. I feel guilty about some things and relieved about others. I don't know if I'm coming or going, so if my moods change in mid gear, please forgive me. I am really glad you're here. It's so nice of you to have come. You didn't have to."

She hung her head again. I could tell that compliments and sincerity made her feel awkward. Considering how young and beautiful she is, that's rather difficult for me to understand.

"Are you sure you want me to stay?" she asked.

"Positive," I told her.

She shot me half a grin.

Just when I was feeling relaxed and comfortable with my new friend, Nurse Nuisance came in to take my pressure again. Stacey sat and watched her closely. When she left, Stacey took out a book and began reading to me. It was a Rip Van Winkle remake, a female version. I found the story interesting, and I loved the way Stacey read it. Her voice fluctuated and she gave each character a distinctive sound. She even gestured and pranced around the room as she read. I had my very own drama queen to entertain me. As she read, I chuckled.

The morning passed by quickly. Stacey had been with me for over two hours before she packed her book away, rubbed my head, and told me to enjoy the rest of my day. My face suddenly felt tight, and the pain in my head returned. I hated to see Stacey leave. I had become instantly dependent upon my new best friend. I felt angry about the fact that someone so wonderful who had just entered my life would soon no longer be a part of it. But, I was also grateful that she and I met. Now that I've met her, I can't imagine having left this life without ever knowing her. She's like an earthly angel who has come to escort me to my heavenly home.

I watched Stacey through saddened eyes as she packed her belongings.

"Can you come by tomorrow," I asked her. She spun around and raised a brow.

"Does that mean I'm not invited to come back later tonight?" she asked.

I could feel my smile stretching across my face.

"You'd come back tonight?" I asked.

"Who else you got to read you a bedtime story," she said as she winked. "Don't you want to hear what happens when the girl wakes up?"

"Yeah," I said. "I'm dying to know what happens next.

The word *dying* struck a sour note for the both of us. We both tried to conceal our feelings as we exchanged phony grins. Stacey came closer to my bed, stood over me for a minute, then kissed my forehead.

"I had a very nice morning," she told me. "I hope you did too."

"Absolutely." I told her. "You promise you'll be back tonight?"

She sashayed her way to the door. "Didn't I say I would?" she teased. "I'll be here," she said more seriously, "I promise. Eat all of your dinner and maybe I'll treat you with dessert."

She winked and waved goodbye. If I died right now, that would be sufficient enough an exit from this world for me.

Chapter 9 - Christine

I never would have thought it, but shopping wasn't the thrill it's made out to be. The first hour was rather exciting, but hunting bargains and trying on clothes in a tiny cubicle just wasn't for me. I got some fancy new pieces that I can't wait to parade myself around in though. I have an appointment to have my hair done in less than thirty minutes.

I hurry to my car, throw my packages in the trunk and speed down Main. It will only take me fifteen minutes to make it to the salon, but speeding is an integral part of my rebellion right now. Yes, I realize that everything I am doing today is in the name of fighting back, but for now, it's the only form of therapy that will help me to recover.

Usually, before I go to a hair salon, I make sure I am equipped with error proofing, distinctive pictures of the kind of cut I want, a hand held mirror to make sure I get the cut I want, and I wig in case someone messes up the cut I want. Today, I have none of that. I'm going into the salon without my weaponry. I will enter with boldness and hopefully exit even more audaciously.

I looked in the mirror and tussled my greasy strands. I smiled as I thought of the transformation that will be made in less that a couple of hours. Everyone says that when you look good, you feel good, and I plan on looking fabulous.

I park my car close to the entrance of Bump A Curl. I shut the ignition off, snatch up my purse, and head into the building that houses my transformation chamber. I see two women leaving as I enter. Both of them are smiling and playing with each other's hair. I make my way to the counter. A young black girl with orange hair greets me.

"Welcome to Bump A Curl," she tells me and smiles.

I grin to conceal my squeamishness at the wad of gum that is oozing its way through her teeth.

"Hi," I tell her. "I have a one o'clock appointment with Sarah." "Sarah," she yells towards the back room. "Your one o'clock is here."

Sarah came from the back. She had apparently been eating lunch because she was using her fingernail as a toothpick. She wiped her hands on her apron and motioned for me as she led the way to her chair. She strolled her big boned body to a corner booth. She pointed to the chair. I sat. Suddenly, I felt a little nervous, but not enough to make me change my mind.

"What you want done?" She asked me.

"Something totally different," I told her. "Short though. I definitely want to have my hair cut short."

She released the bobby pins from my hair and stretched my hair down to its full length.

"You want all this cut?" she asked. "Yup. Take it

off," I told her.

"Dang!" she said. "Who you mad at?" "What do you mean?" I asked her.

"When a woman comes in and asks that her long hair be cut off, and she doesn't have a particular style in mind, she's mad at somebody. Cutting hair symbolizes cutting something or someone out of your life. The equation is normally all messed up. One and one don't equal *one* no more. Something puts it back in its place and makes it two again." She winked.

Sarah pulled more strands of my hair out and grunted, "Ummm, humph. You mad at somebody."

I didn't answer, but I gave her a smile that let her know her summation was right.

"So," she said, "you leaving this craftsmanship up to me, huh?" I looked at her hair, short, silky, and neatly curled, not a strand out of place.

"Yup," I answered, "It's all up to you. Make me look…"

"I got you girl," she interrupted. "You want a make your man wanna cry and beg you to take him back kinda do."

We both smiled.

"Something like that." I said.

"Well let's get to it then." She told me.

Sarah worked on my hair for almost an hour, shampooing twice, conditioning three times, clearing it out, cutting it up, wrapping it around, and spritzing it like mad. I sat under her heat wave of a dryer for over an hour more. Within minutes of sitting in Sarah's chair, which she deliberately faced away from her mirror, she had curled and styled me into a goddess. When she spun me around to see my reflection, I hardly noticed myself. I was beautiful. Suddenly, I felt a calming and a gentleness come over me. I thought I would cry. Sarah, unable to read my expressions clearly, raised her eyebrows and asked,

"So, what do you think?"

"I love it." I told her. "I really, really love it."

She smiled real big and started playing with my curls.

"You do look good." She told me. "I think I've outdone myself," she teased.

"Yes, you have," I told her. "You certainly have."

I hugged Sarah like she was a long lost friend and left her a hefty tip. She told me to be sure to come back and see her again. That's a request that will definitely be honoured.

On my way out the door I heard women commenting on how good my hair looked. Others displayed envy and shot me the you- must-think-you're-cute-now look. I accepted both as compliments and went out the door with my head held high. I felt better than I have in years.

As soon as I hopped in the car, I looked at myself again in the mirror, and later I found myself looking in anything that showed my reflection for most of the day, store window, car windows, and compacts. Seeing my change on the outside caused me to feel a distinct change on the inside. I felt confident, powerful, and energetic. I was ready to face the world. But first, I would face someone else. I wanted to share my new look.

While my makeup was fresh and my hairdo was striking, I thought I would go and visit the reverend. I wanted desperately for him to see my hair and to admire the new me. Once again, I stepped on the gas and drove well over the speed limit. I wanted to arrive at my destination in a flash. Even though the red lights annoyed me, it was nice to look over and see men admiring me from their cars. Each time, I turned away to shield my blush.

I arrived at the reverend's in minimum time. When I got there, I saw approximately ten cars in the yard. I had obviously arrived at a bad time, but I desperately wanted to see the reverend, or to put it more accurately, I desperately wanted him to see me. I decided to call him on my cell phone to let him know I was outside. I just needed him to escape from his company long enough to see the new me. I dialed his number. He answered on the first ring. He has caller ID, so I took that as a good sign.

"Hello, Christine," he said in a bubbly tone.

"Hi there, Revvy," I said, mocking his niece Stacey.

"Everything alright?" he asked.

"Why don't you come outside and see," I told him.

I caught him looking out of the living room window. It took him a couple of seconds, but he finally spotted my car. He hung up and came right out. I smiled wide as he approached my window. I wound it down and looked at him seductively.

"So, what do you think?" I asked him. "Like my hair?"

He was speechless, but his expression told

me he thought I looked stunning.

"Wow, what brought on such a change?" he asked.

"Lots of changes will be taking place in my life from now on," I told him. "Charles moved out last night."

Again, he was speechless.

"Moved out...of the house, you mean? Left you? Is that what you're saying?"

"That's what I'm saying," I said and smiled.

"You appear to be handling it well," he told me.

I grinned. "So, What's going on in there?" I asked him.

He hesitated and started stumbling, but he finally got it out,

"It's a birthday party for my wife."

I was confused.

"Your wife? But your wife is..." I couldn't say the word.

"Yeah, but it's a tradition. She loved birthday parties so much that I still give one for her every year. The family comes by, we eat cake, talk about her, look at her pictures. It makes us all feel pretty good." He said. I could tell he was a bit uncomfortable about sharing the information with me.

"Oh, that's so thoughtful. You must have really loved her," was all I could manage. I couldn't believe I was jealous of a deceased woman.

"Well, you'd better get back to the party. I'm sorry to have intruded."

I was sure my face was a good olive shade by now. "Maybe I'll give you a call a little later," I told him.

"That would be nice," he said so formally that it made me feel embarrassed.

"Your hair looks great and the makeup is nice," he told me. His acknowledging what now seemed a trivial reason for stopping by made me feel even more ashamed and very school girlish.

I smirked, rolled up my window, and slowly drove down the hill of his driveway. On the way down, I passed Stacey. I waved. She cut her eyes and continued up the hill. I was baffled by her attitude, but I decided not to try to analyze it. Instead, I began my journey on the long and scenic route home. Even after my full day, I was in no hurry to get back to my empty house.

It took me almost forty-five minutes to travel what could have been a twenty-five minute distance. I took my packages out of the car and decided I would entertain myself for the next couple of minutes by pretending I was Tyra Banks with a better do. Before heading upstairs to my room, I checked the phone for messages. Charles had called four times and left four voice messages. He expressed each time how much he hoped I was "managing alright", reminding me of the cash he left for me, which has already been spent, and telling me he loves me. I haven't heard him say that so much since we got married. I tried to locate the number he had called from, but he was sure to block it each time. A part of me wished I had been at home to receive at least one of the calls. I still had a lot of questions that needed to be answered, but another part of me was glad I wasn't around to receive them. I needed to get out and enjoy myself without heavy thoughts of Charles weighing on my mind.

I spent nearly an hour pretending I was a supermodel. I looked good in everything I'd bought. Charles's money had definitely been well spent. After I packed the clothes away, I sat on the edge of my bed and tried to come up with a plan for the remainder of my night. I didn't like the fact that I had no idea what to do with myself. I decided to fix a light snack. My appetite still wasn't quite right. I went to the kitchen to find something that would satisfy my palate. After digging through each of the cupboards and the refrigerator twice, I couldn't pinpoint anything I really had a taste for, so I settled for just a hot cup of tea instead.

I found a book I had begun reading a couple of weeks ago and decide to continue it. I was five pages into it when the phone rang.

The caller ID read "Blocked."

"Yes," I answered snootily.

"Hi, Chris. I've been trying to call you all day," Charles said.

"Yeah, I see. I know how to pass time, Charles. I rather enjoy my own company," I hissed.

"Well, I'm glad you're doing alright. You sound good."

"What did you think I was going to do, Charles, sit around and mope at the fact that you're gone? Did you think I would be sitting her crying a river?" I gallantly asked him.

He ignored my questions.

"Chris, I really need to talk to you. There are things we need to discuss," he said.

"Yeah, Charles, you're right, but I'm not up for any discussions right now," I told him.

"When do you think you might be ready to talk, Chris?" he asked.

"Charles," I told him. "I've been ready to talk with you for years. That's all I've been trying to do. I wanted to talk about us, our marriage, about what went wrong, about how we could prevent things from getting worse. You told me that you didn't want to talk. You snubbed me, now you're asking me when I'd be ready to talk. I don't know, Charles. I don't feel much like talking any more."

"I know I've hurt you, Chris. I realize that all of this is my fault.

I want the chance to make things up to you. I need to see you. It's important." He sounded sincere, but I wasn't ready to give in, not yet.

"So tell me, Charles, where are you? Off somewhere still being taken care of?" I asked him.

"Yes, I'm…," he started.

Suddenly, I heard a woman in the background. I listened closely.

"Hey, there, Sporty. I'm back and I hope you ate all your dinner, because I got your dessert," she told him and giggled. "Oh, sorry, I didn't realize you were on the phone," she added.

Her voice sounded familiar, but I couldn't identify it.

"Well, Charles," I said, "Your *dessert* is waiting for you. You'd better go before it loses its sweetness."

Charles knew I was irritated and I knew he was uncomfortable. "I'll call you again tomorrow, okay?" he told me.

"Don't bother," I told him before slamming down the phone.

I was irate. I poured the remains of my tea down the sink and packed up my book. I went straight to the bathroom and filled the tub. I needed Calgon to take me away.

Chapter 10 - Charles

Through all of Christine's sarcasm, all I could really hear was pain. No matter what she says, I'll keep calling until she accepts my invitation to talk. I hate thinking about having to tell her I'm dying. Even though she's angry with me right now, Chris and I have a past, a good one, and we are after all, still husband and wife.

I love Christine and I should have shown her that more instead of focusing on myself. I should have been more attentive to her. Maybe that was all the medicine I needed to make me feel better. The painkillers I took didn't kill the pain. They just numbed me for a while. Christine's coldness towards me is taking the same effect.

I looked over at Stacey who was taking her book out of her purse.

"Sorry," she said. "I didn't notice you were on the phone."

"No big deal." I told her. I knew she was curious, so I went ahead and added, "I was talking to Christine."

Stacey twisted up her mouth and grunted.

"You ready to hear the rest of your story?" she asked. "I got your dessert here too, carrot cake. I bet you're ready for that."

I smiled and reached my hand out to accept the bag. I took a bite of the cake.

"Mmm. Oh yeah! Alright, I'm ready. Read."

Stacey smiled a pleased smile. My drama queen continued her performance from this morning in the same manner, gesturing, prancing around, and changing voices. She read like a pro and brought that story to life. She was something to watch, womanly beautiful with a child-like playfulness.

Stacey had been reading for just over an hour when the nurse came in to check my pressure. I crumpled my dessert bag and threw it in a corner. I wiped my mouth to make sure no trace of carrot cake icing was on it. Stacey chuckled at my badness. I winked at her. The nurse caught me winking, but somehow thought my wink was aimed at her. She blushed.

"Okay, Mr. Freshy pants," she said, "You're fine. Looking good."

When she left, Stacey and I laughed. That's something I haven't done in a long time.

Stacey stayed for about thirty minutes longer before telling me she needed to head home. As she packed her book away, Stacey asked, "You thought any more about letting your wife know where you are?"

"Still thinking on it," I told her. "I don't want Christine to come while she's so upset. She's going through a lot right now."

"Humph," Stacey grunted. "She don't seem too upset to me."

She spun around and looked at me like a child who had just been caught being bad.

"What do you mean?" I asked her. "Don't pay me no mind," she said.

"You seen Christine?" I pressed. "You said she don't seem too upset to you. You must have seen her. Where was she?"

Stacey didn't answer. That was answer enough.

"Was she visiting your uncle again? Is that where you saw her?" Again, her silence spoke volumes. She gave me a cheerless look.

"Hey, don't worry about it," I told her. "I should've guessed it." "Sorry," Stacey said. "I didn't mean to make you feel bad. Sometimes my mouth runs faster than my brain can catch it."

"Hey," I said, "Quit guilt trippin'. You haven't said or done anything wrong. You've been great. You've helped me to survive my first day in here. I'm grateful to you. I don't mean to sound pushy, but I hope you come again. No pressure. Just if you have time, I mean. I'd like to see you again. Maybe hear another story. You're a fabulous reader. I could listen to your stories all day. You sure you're heading into the right profession? You could give all those top actresses a run for their money."

Stacey blushed and hid her face, shunning yet another compliment.

"Charmer," She said. "I had fun today too. I'll definitely be back to see you again. I'll come tomorrow. I'm not sure what time. I've got to meet with Doc Kaylor in the morning for a couple of of hours, but I'm free during the afternoon. Think you could survive without me for that long?"

"I'll try," I told her.

She came over to my bed, rubbed my head, totally messing up my hair, and tapped my nose.

"See you tomorrow, Sunshine. You gonna be alright?"

"I'm a big boy," I told her.

"I'll be fine."

"If you need anything," she winked, "Holla for your girlfriend out there." She nudged her head towards the nurse's station and giggled.

"Very funny," I told her and giggled too.

As Stacey made her way out the door, I felt a sudden sadness come over me. I laid in bed and reflected on how sad my life has been lately, and I thought of ways I could make my last days better. Christine came to mind. In order for me to start liking myself a little more, I would definitely have to amend things with Christine. After much pondering, I came to the conclusion that the best thing I could do for Chris was to give her a gift, and I knew exactly what it was she would value most…her freedom.

I guess sometimes it takes putting oneself last in order to put someone else first. So, in losing this race, I guess I'm actually winning. Hopefully, my sacrifice will erase some of my sins.

I closed my eyes to pray. I prayed for peace of mind, direction, and wisdom. I prayed for guidance in dealing with Christine. I prayed that she would be able to forgive me for being such a terrible husband, and I prayed that I would be able to forgive myself. Most of all, because I've got so many preparations to make, I prayed that I wouldn't be closing my eyes for the last time any time soon.

Chapter 11 - Charles

Last night was the worst night of my life. A collage of scenes from my life flashed through my mind one behind the other like a movie on manual fast forward. I saw myself as a boy having pillow fights with my brothers and sisters. I saw my favourite teacher, Mrs. Mackey patting my head. I saw my daddy in the yard raking up leaves and telling me to fetch him a cool glass of water. I saw my mama singing in the choir at church and winking at me after she'd hit a high note. I saw myself running in the park with Paulette, my first girlfriend ever. I saw myself at my high school graduation, my college graduation, and applying for my first job as a shelf stocker at K-Mart. I saw Barclay, my Golden Retriever licking my face, and I saw Christine, looking as beautiful as ever on our wedding day. I could feel myself smiling in my sleep.

But then, something woke me up...and kept me up. It was seeing my grandma Cassie, my brother Butch, and my daddy in their coffins. Even though they were buried in different states, in my dream, they were lying side by side, and I was lying right there beside them. Each of them lay there peacefully with their eyes closed and with a half a grin on their faces. I sat up in my coffin and looked them over. I tried to close my eyes, cross my arms about me, and find the kind of peace they had found, but it wouldn't happen.

Then, someone shut off the air supply and I found it harder and harder to breathe. I panicked, looked around for someone to save me, but all I saw was Christine's face going in and out of focus in front of me. She looked at me with pity and although I didn't see any tears coming from her eyes, I could hear her crying.

I heard a voice calling out to me. I was sure of it, but each time I opened my eyes to answer, I met with silence and darkness. Beads of sweat rolled down face and my back. I wanted to scream out of both fear and frustration. As I lay awake, everything I needed to do to amend situations in my life became clearer and clearer to me.

I could no longer prolong things. I had to make changes, adjustments, reparations, and I had to do it all now. I can't go peacefully if I leave things undone. I don't know how much time I have left, so I need to make use of every minute. I had phone calls to make and letters to write.

I asked the nurse at the station for a couple of sheets of paper and a pen. I began my first letter. I felt a sense of relief after I had written it. Such a huge weight had already been lifted off my shoulders, and that prompted me to write my next one. By the time I was done, I had written seven lengthy personal letters and quite a few shorter ones to banks and companies. I needed envelopes and stamps. I called Stacey and asked her to bring me some. She told me she wouldn't be coming to see me until after three o'clock. She had some work to do at Dr. Kaylor's office. That left me with plenty of time to call Christine.

I suddenly wanted Christine to know how much I love her and I wanted to tell her so without holding back. I wanted to vent to her the way I had done in my letters. I dialed my home phone. I was surprised by what I heard on the other end. It was a recording stating, "The number you have dialed has been disconnected or is no longer in service. If you feel you have reached this recording in error, hang up and try your call again." I did just that. I hung up and tried my call again. This time, I dialed slowly, watching my fingers deliberately press each digit. Without ringing, I heard the voice I'd heard only seconds ago, parroting the same message. "The number you have dialed…" I hung up. Either Christine hadn't paid the bill or she was going out of her way to pay me no mind.

I called the telephone company, gave them my name, social security number, and mother's maiden name as confirmation that it was truly me on the other end requesting information about my own phone line. The patient woman who was working with me informed me that the number had been changed and that her computer screen showed that my name had been taken off the bill. Christine was on her way to self-assertion. A part of me was angry, but another part of me was proud of her. I thanked the operator for her assistance, put the phone down, shook my head and smiled.

Even though not being able to get in touch with Christine dampened my spirits a little, I decided that I would enjoy today. For the first time, since I've been hospitalized, I've decided to make the most of my situation. I'll thankfully eat the tasteless food. I'll let the ugly nurse wheel me around outside and take me for a "walk". I'll select items from the hospitality cart, and I'll finally watch the TV my insurance is paying for, and when Stacey comes to visit, I'll read to *her*. I'll take a longer shower, and I'll even wash my hair. Then, I'll hang out at the nurse's station and flirt a little. But before I do all of that, I have to write one more letter. My wife needs to know what's on my mind.

I drafted a letter to Christine, and then I read it and re-read it. What I had written down was sincere, and it sounded like poetry.

I was proud of myself. I put all of my letters on the end table near my bed, placed my feet firmly on the ground and headed to the bathroom to shower. The water running down my back felt like warm tears flowing from Heaven. I finally felt like God was pleased with me again. I started to sing. I sang, *"God Has Smiled On Me."* I didn't know all the words, but I made some up as I went along.

I lathered up all over and put some soap in my hair. My bar of odorless Ivory smelled like gardenias. I turned the water on full blast, stood directly under the hose, and submerged myself completely, baptizing myself.

I closed my eyes, felt the water trickling down my body and prayed. I prayed harder than I had in a long time. I wanted to make sure God knew me again and was proud to call me His son.

As I stepped out of the bathroom with the steam behind me, I suddenly felt even more steam coming from my ears. Seated in the visitor's corner of my room was the last person I would have expected to see, Reverend Baxter. He was in *my* room, but he looked like he was just as surprised to see me as I was to see him. He stood.

"What are you doing here?" I asked him.

"I came to see you. They called me." He answered.

"*They*?" I asked him.

"Who's *they*?"

"The doctors," he began, "They told me about your condition.

They said," he hesitated "…They said you didn't have much longer," he whispered.

"They did, did they? Hmm." I responded disdainfully.

I'd forgotten about all the initial paperwork *they* made me fill out upon arrival. There was a portion that asked about religious affiliations and such.

"God's the only one who knows how much time I got," I told him. "Ain't that right, Rev?" I mocked.

"What's going on, Charles? I had no idea you were ill," he said. "I'm not ill," I told him. "Ill is what you are when you have a cold. I don't have a cold. I won't be getting over this. I'm not ill. I'm sick. What I have is terminal. That fits well with your plans, now doesn't it?" I glared at him. He hung his head.

"Does Christine know? She hasn't said anything…" he stopped.

"I guess she's got other things on her mind when she's with you," I told him.

He kept his eyes on the floor and fumbled with his hat.

"No," I confessed. "Christine doesn't know. She has no idea. She doesn't even know I'm in here. Unless you told her, that is."

He looked surprised and started stuttering,

"Nnn…nnn…no, I didn't tell her. I came right over when I was called. Why?…How come…Christine doesn't know?"

I didn't feel like talking to the sanctimonious wife stealer who had invaded my room and rained on my parade before the first beating of the drum. I went to the end table where my letters lay and pulled out the one I had written to him. It explained it all, the Mesothelioma, my attitude, my marital woes, my love for Christine, and the reasons I didn't want her to know about my condition. I even left instructions for him on how to tend to my wife when I'm gone. I revealed the fact that I knew about him and Christine. I felt like I had just handed the man ownership papers, like I was transferring my whole life over to him.

While he read, I dressed. I probably should have gone into the bathroom to do so, but I already felt naked and exposed. The Reverend took longer to read the letter than it took me to write it. He must have read it several times to make sure its meaning was clear and to make sure that the words he thought he was seeing on the pages were really there. When he was done, he looked up at me with pitiful eyes. He folded the letter and put it in his pocket.

"I'm sorry, Charles. I'm really very sorry. I don't know what to say. Aside from what you've noted in the letter, is there anything I can do for you? Anything at all?" He asked.

I felt like telling him that staying away from my wife would be a start. Instead, I shot him down with a flat, "No."

The room was silent. Neither of us knew what to say and neither of us had the gumption enough to look the other in the eye. I went to my window and looked outside.

"Don't you tell Christine I'm here. I don't care how close you feel to her, it's not your place. She's still my wife, and as far as I'm concerned, you've interfered in my marriage enough. I'll tell Christine everything she needs to know when I'm ready. You mind your business, you got that Rev?" I asked him.

"Yeah," he whispered. "I understand. I really am sorry, Charles."

I had no intentions of letting him off easy.

"Sorry for what?" I asked him. I was looking at him now. "Sorry that I'm sick? Sorry that you've stolen my wife? Or are you sorry that you stole my wife before you found out that I was sick? What exactly is it that you're sorry for?"

He hung his head again. I heard him sniffle and I saw him swallow hard.

"You gonna be able to handle everything I wrote in your note?" I asked him in a more composed manner.

"Are you sure you want me to?" was his response.

I hesitated. "Yeah," I told him. "I think it's best."

He didn't answer. He took the note out of his pocket, scanned it, folded it up and placed it in his pocket again. He put his hat on and ambled over to me. He held out his hand. I looked at it for a while before accepting it.

Once I did, he pulled me to him and hugged me tight. I was suddenly reminded of the day I took out membership in the church. His hug felt the same. That day marked the beginning of a great friendship between us. I guess everything really does come full circle. We both had tears in our eyes and frogs in our throats. We silently agreed that no more words were necessary. He turned away from me and slowly started to head out of my door. Just like Lot's wife, he couldn't help himself. He looked back. I saluted him. He tipped his hat and saluted me. I watched him leave. As I did, my stomach pains returned. Reality was coming back to greet me.

Chapter 12 - Christine

I was in the kitchen scrubbing the tile floor when I heard a knock on the door that startled me. I wasn't expecting anyone, so I looked out of the window to see who it could be. I was stunned to see Reverend Baxter's car parked in my driveway. My heart started beating rapidly and my hands started to shake. I felt like a schoolgirl. I looked at myself in the hallway mirror. I was a mess. I was wearing clothes that didn't match, I reeked of Clorox, and my fancy do was tied down with an old, red bandana. I didn't have on any shoes. My toes were exposed, showing patches of chipped polish. I wanted to run upstairs and hide, but the reverend's knock persisted. I was sure he knew I was inside, so I reluctantly went to the door and cracked it just a bit.

"Reverend, Hi. I wasn't expecting you," I said to him.

"Hi, Christine. I know this visit is totally unannounced, but you mind if I come in for a minute?" he asked. "I tried calling but..." he didn't finish his sentence. He just shot me a curious grin.

After all the times I've popped in on him lately, I couldn't very well say no. I opened the door all the way. He looked me over, but somehow, I got the feeling he didn't really see me. He looked disturbed.

"Everything alright?" I asked him, wondering why he had come.

"Yes," he said.   "Fine."

I could tell that was a lie, but I didn't want to push him. "Can I get you something? A cup of tea maybe?" I asked.

He quickly accepted. "Tea would be nice. Thank you."

I sent him into the living room where he could make himself more comfortable. I removed my gloves and washed my hands well before preparing his hot cup of Earl Grey. From time to time as the water heated, I glanced into the living room and watched the reverend's movements. They were slow and deliberate. Even though it hadn't changed much since the last time he was over, he walked around the living room, like he had been in it for the first time. He found a picture of Charles and me. One I hadn't gotten around to boxing up yet. He examined it closely. Something was definitely going on inside the reverend's head. The kettle whistled to me that it was time to find out what that was.

I put the tea on my finest silver tray and added a plate of cookies, some after dinner mints and a couple of napkins. I searched the cabinets for other goodies, but there weren't any. These would have to do.

"Tea time," I sang as I entered the living room.

I placed the tray on the coffee table and motioned for the reverend to have a seat on the sofa. "So," I asked him, "what brings you by?" I scooted closer to him. "Not that you need a reason, of course." I winked.

He gave a forced crooked smile and answered, "I was worried about you. I thought I'd come and find out how you're handling things."

"Things?" I asked him. "What things? The house? My finances? My emotions? The fact that my husband just up and left me? What things exactly are you referring to?" I teased. Before he could answer, I continued, "As you can see, I'm handling things just fine. The house is still standing, my finances though gradually declining, are in order, my emotional state has drastically improved, and the fact that my husband has left me has proven beneficial to my personal growth. I feel more in control of myself than I have in a long time. I'm through crying. You won't see me shedding any more tears. So, how am I handling things? I'm handling things just fine, thank you." By this time, my attitude had changed. I could feel my face getting flushed and I could hear the sarcasm in my tone. The reverend noticed too.

He took my hand in his and massaged it a little.

"I'm here for you," he told me. "You might need me in the very near future, and when you find you do, don't hesitate to call upon me day or night. I want you to understand that."

Something was very disturbing about his mood. The more I sat with Reverend Baxter the more edgy I became.

I didn't answer him. Instead, I reached for the teapot and poured two cups. We sat and drank our tea in silence for what felt like an eternity. I had to do something to break the deafening silence, but I wasn't sure what. I decided to ask the reverend for help loading my packed boxes into a corner of my garage. Even though he was dressed in a suit, he saw I needed help and gladly accepted. He took off his jacket and laid it across the arm of the sofa. He undid his tie and laid it there also. Within minutes, he managed to tote three boxes back and forth. I was impressed by his masculinity. I smiled as I watched him maneuver in and out of my back door with my heavy packages. He caught me a couple of times and bashfully smiled back. I had only two boxes left.

"Can you manage the rest or am I becoming a slave driver?" I asked him.

"Nah. I'm fine. I can manage," he told me.

He snatched up the next box, which must not have been tightly secured. Just as he was making his way towards the door, the bottom of the box busted and all of the contents fell to the floor. Like some type of omen, that box contained the many albums of pictures of Charles and me. Scenes from my life were suddenly splattered all over the place.

I got down on my knees to gather them up. The reverend rushed to help me. While I busied myself re-taping the box, Reverend Baxter seemed to grow more and more engrossed in my past life. He scanned pictures of Charles and me during our courtship, at our wedding, at family and church functions, and taking studio shots. He began to inquire about a couple of them. I sat on the floor beside him and recapped those portions of my life. Reverend Baxter appeared genuinely interested in knowing so much about my life with Charles. At times, I found his line of questioning rather intrusive, but I answered him nonetheless.

Recalling some of my better days with Charles made me a sentimental fool. Tears started to fall. I tried to control them and to assert myself the way I had done just moments earlier, but I couldn't help myself and I was forced to surrender to them.

Reverend Baxter quickly placed the half taped box and the pictures on the floor and helped me to my feet. He took a napkin off the tray and offered it to me. I held it in my hand, but didn't have the strength to dry my own tears. All the feelings I had shoved inside and refused to vent came out. I bawled like a wounded animal. Reverend Baxter stood motionless and stared at me in alarm. He finally put his arms around me and held me close. I needed that. I needed him.

I reached up and tightly held onto his neck. I pressed my cheek against his and soaked his collar with my tears. He just stood there and held me firmly. He was my rock, my fortress. In between my wails, I could hear the reverend whispering apologies. I paid no attention. I just held on and blubbered until I was tired.

As my cries grew faint, Reverend Baxter eased my arms from around his neck and led me to the sofa. He sat beside me. Neither of us spoke. Our silence had come full circle.

He stretched me out and put a pillow under my head. He uncomfortably positioned himself on the edge. He stroked my head and told me to go ahead and fall asleep.

"It would do you some good to get a little rest," he told me.

I didn't fight him. I closed my eyes and pictured tulips and puppies. I saw myself in a rocking chair on my front porch. I had a puppy in my lap. A child came and stroked it. The child smiled and reached up to kiss me on the cheek. I bent down to make it easier for her to do. The puppy jumped out of my lap and ran down the stairs and into the tall grass that was growing in my yard. The little girl ran after him. I watched them and beamed with delight.

Then, a man appeared at the screen door behind me. He came outside and handed me a cool glass of pink lemonade. He stood beside me and stroked my head. My life was beautiful. I looked up at the man. He was tall and statuesque. I could tell he was beautiful, but I couldn't see his face. He continued to stroke my head. I reached up and held onto his hand. My face rested on his arm. I sighed and shifted. I opened my eyes. Reverend Baxter looked at me and smiled.

"Hey there," he said. "Feeling any better?"

"Yeah," I answered. I was confused. I must have been dreaming, but the pictures in my head were so real. Nonetheless, I was glad the reverend was still with me. I sat up and looked around. My living room, which was in disarray when I fell asleep, was now orderly.

"You cleaned up a little, huh?" I asked him. "Yeah, just a bit. You really need to relax. You've been under a lot of pressure. I'm here now and I can help.

Will you let me?"

I didn't know how to answer. I wanted to say, "Yes", but I didn't want to appear weak. I had an image to uphold, one of independence, determination, and self-assertion. I didn't want anyone's pity. "I…", I started, but was suddenly stopped mid sentence by a delectable aroma.

"Do you smell food?" I asked the reverend.

"Actually," he smiled, "I do."

"Had I started cooking before I fell asleep?" I confusedly asked.

I was sure I hadn't, but I was still a little disoriented and my mind still wasn't quite clear, so I knew anything was possible.

"No. I…I hope you don't mind, but I thought you might be hungry when you woke, so I started dinner for you," he answered nervously.

I was totally shocked. "You started dinner?"

"Yes…I had no right in your kitchen, I know, but…I just…well, I…I…I hope you're not upset." His hands were shaking and he looked flushed. I wasn't used to this kind of treatment. I didn't know how to respond. Suddenly, my throat felt tight and my hands got clammy.

"No, I'm not upset, I just…well…that was very sweet of you. I've never….No one's ever…I…" I felt like a bumbling idiot. I stared into the reverend's gentle eyes. I wanted to hold him in my arms and love him. We sat together for a minute while silence became our friend again.

After a couple of awkward minutes, I cleared my throat and said, "Well, let's find out what's cooking. I'm hungry all of a sudden."

The reverend smiled. He stood first, and then extended his hand to help me up. He continued to hold my hand as he led me to the kitchen. I loved the way he was taking full control. He lifted the top off of the boiling pot. The kitchen was filled with a mouthwatering smell.

"Umm, umm!" I said as I shut my eyes and took a whiff. As the reverend stirred the contents of the pot, I took a peek inside. I spotted whole potatoes, large chunks of fresh carrots, bell pepper quarters, cubes of beef and more.

"You had all the right stuff to make stew the way my mama used to," he told me. "I was hoping that if you liked it enough, you would want to show your gratitude by allowing a hungry man like me to partake in this meal with you," he teased.

"When my neigbour is hungry, it's my duty to feed him, and when my neighbour thirsts, I will give him a drink," I teased back. I smiled through the tears of joy I worked desperately to hold back. I was overwhelmed.

"How much longer will we have to wait until it's ready?" I asked.

The reverend stirred the pot again. "It appears to be just about done."

"That's what I was hoping you'd say." I told him. "While you continue to keep an eye on the food, I'll go and wash up. I need to change into some more fitting clothes also, but I won't take long. I'll be just a minute."

I dashed upstairs, smiling all the way. As I passed the hallway mirror, I stopped to look at myself. Instead of seeing a 38 year old, nearly wrinkled, sour faced, husband rejected, hag, I saw a bubbly teenager in pigtails. One who had just been kissed. I ran to my closet, and snatched down a casual dress. Then I went to my drawer and pulled out some fresh underwear. I went to my vanity and collected bath gel, powder, Secret, and my nearly empty bottle of Estee Lauder *Pleasures* perfume. I checked the clock. It was 5:57 p.m. I would take no more than fifteen minutes to transform myself into a beautiful swan.

I went into the bathroom, ran warm bath water, put in a couple of drops of gel, and undressed as quickly as I could. When I got into the bath, the water felt so tantalizing that I wanted to soak for hours, but the thought of the great meal that had been prepared for me and the wonderful man I would be sharing it with motivated me to speed it up. I washed well, dressed quickly, powdered up, put on my Secret, and sprayed two shots of *Pleasures* into my cleavage. I untied my new do and ran my fingers through my short mane, fluffing it a little. In seconds it was sexy. I loved my new cut.

I did a once over in the mirror. I beamed at my beauty. I was ready, and I hoped the reverend was ready for me. It was my mission to show that man my gratitude. As I packed up my grungies, I checked the clock. It was 6:13. Not bad.

I went downstairs, and made my entrance with a fashion model stride. I smiled a smile that said, "Eat your heart out 'cause I know I look good." The reverend looked me over from head to toe. He froze in position.

"Wow," he said, "You clean up real good, Christine. Real good." I gloried in his calling me by my name. It always sounded so sweet rolling off his tongue. I smiled a modest smile.

"Thanks," I said bashfully as I patted down my hair.

"Well," he said as he hooked his arm around mine and escorted me to the dining room, "Ready to eat?"

I was suddenly nervous and I had lost my appetite, but I wouldn't dare let it show.

"I'm famished," I lied.

The reverend smiled, seated me, and retired to the kitchen.

Hearing him clanking dishes and pouring drinks made me feel special. A fine man was serving me a fine meal. No woman on earth had it better than me.

Hearing him clanking dishes and pouring drinks made me feel special. A fine man was serving me a fine meal. No woman on earth had it better than me. So many emotions were taking over at once. I was on a first date in my own uncontrolled environment. Just as I closed my eyes to silently ask God to help me through the night, the reverend emerged from the kitchen with our meals on a tray. The tray had been adorned with a vase and one of the lilies from my garden.

"I hope you don't mind that I plucked one of your flowers from its bed. I thought adding the lily would be a nice touch," he said.

"It's perfect," I told him, "Just like everything else you've done so far."

He blushed and laid the tray on the table. He moved his chair closer to mine and sat. He took my hand in his and bowed his head. I followed his lead.

He prayed over the food and thanked God that the two of us were able to be company for each other.

Then, he picked up *my* fork and offered me the first bite of food. I couldn't believe he cooked the meal on his own. I chewed slowly, savoring every delectable bite.

The dinner was scrumptious, the company was beautiful, and the conversation was engaging. I felt like I was in Heaven. With both my stomach and my heart full, I sat in my seat, planted well and unable to move. The reverend stood to clear the table. I felt guilty and offered to take on the job of cleaning up. He wouldn't allow it. He insisted I remain seated. He told me that the best was yet to come.

I hear the reverend fumbling around in the kitchen for a couple of minutes. Then, he returned to the dining room, carrying the silver tray I had used at teatime. On the tray were fresh slices of fruit neatly decorated on a plate and a bowl of some type of whipped topping. There was also the teapot and two cups.

"Got room for dessert?" he asked.

"Goodness, you made dessert too?" I asked.

"No dinner would be complete without it," he winked. "It's nothing fancy, just some fruit and cream. Although, I must add that I made the cream myself. I used some of your eggs and a heaping of your sugar. I owe you some groceries."

I smiled. "Well, I told him. You should have warned me to save room. I don't know if I can eat another bite."

"Come on," he urged. "A couple of slices of fruit won't hurt."

He took a quarter of an orange off of the plate, swiped it through the bowl of cream, and put it to my lips. I tasted its sweetness. It was delicious. I motioned for him to feed me some more. He smiled and moved closer to me, placing the tray on the table directly between us. He picked up a strawberry and repeated the same gestures he had made with the orange. I wanted to repay the favour, so I reached for a piece of fruit and fed him too. The plate of fruit disappeared far too quickly for me. With every bite I took, I became more and more enraptured with the reverend.

I was incredibly full now and my heart was overflowing. The reverend sat and stared at me with a penetrating gaze. I broke the silence.

"Thanks for dinner and dessert. For helping me out earlier, for cleaning up my mess in both the dining room and the kitchen. Thanks for babysitting me today. I couldn't have asked for better company or to have had a better time. I'm a lucky woman. You're a great friend," I thought it safe to become more familiar with him, so I concluded my thanks by calling him by his name, "Conrad." Conrad smiled. I could tell he was pleased.

Conrad stood slowly. "Thank you, Christine," he said, "For letting me invade your space for so long and for allowing me to totally take charge of your kitchen. It's been quite some time since I've had someone to cook for. Stacey rarely eats at home. She's always on the go. I had a good time today. The best I've had in years. Isn't it funny how the simple things in life, like sharing a meal with a friend, is the most therapeutic and most beautiful thing one can do? Today has meant a lot to me,

Christine, and I hope it's meant something to you too. I wish this day didn't have to end."

That was all I needed to hear. I got up from my seat and stood directly in front of him. I looked him dead in the eyes and mustered up enough courage to respond in a way I have wanted to for some time now, "It doesn't have to, Conrad. Please stay."

He froze in position, which put me in the driver's seat. I decided that the ultimate way of showing Conrad my thanks was by granting him his wish. I leaned in closer to him. I put my hand behind his neck and pulled his face into mine. I tasted his lips. What started as a nibble turned harsh and ravenous. Suddenly, we both had healthy appetites again.

Chapter 13 – Charles

It's been almost a week since I've seen the reverend. I've been torturing myself ever since, wondering whether or not he has exposed my secret to Christine. I wish I knew how to contact my wife by phone. My time is drawing near. I can feel it. I can't eat, sleep, or sit upright for long without my stomach paining me. I think my body has become immune to the drugs the nurses keep feeding me.

Each time I close my eyes, my daddy, my brother and my grandma come clearer and clearer into focus. And now, I have identified the voice that keeps calling out to me in my dreams. It's the voice of God. I'm sure of it. He's letting me know my room is ready and that my number will be called soon. Aside from making sure Christine will be alright and letting her know how much I love her and how sorry I am for the way our marriage turned out, I'm ready to meet my maker. I'm ready to see my God face to face.

Just as the nurse comes in to check my pressure and my pulse for the fourth time today, she finds me balled up on the edge of my bed. She lifts me gently and stretches me out. She puts the covers over me and tells me to rest. She presses the call button on the side of my bed and dials the nurse's station.

"Call Dr. Kaylor," she tells the nurse who answers. "She needs to come and see Mr. Rutherford right away. And call his reverend too, the one who was here the other day. His name and number are listed on his chart."

I grabbed her arm and spoke through my pain, "Don't call him. I don't need to see him."

"Who?" she asked, "Your reverend? You don't want to see your reverend?"

"No," I told her. "I don't need to see him."

"Mr. Rutherford," she said sympathetically, "Your time is short. Didn't they explain that to you in therapy the other day? Didn't the psychiatrist warn you? I think you might need your clergyman."

"The psychiatrist told me to make my final wishes known," I snapped. "I'm making it known that I don't want to see him. Don't call my...*him*. I've already seen him and everything I had to say to him I've already said."

The nurse confusedly looked at me. Then, she hesitantly pressed the call button again. "Cancel calling the reverend," she told the voice that answered. The voice agreed to do so and added, "Doctor Kaylor will be here around noon."

The nurse, suddenly remembering why she had paid me a visit, reached for her stethoscope and conducted business as usual. Just as she was making her exit, Stacey bounced into the room. The nurse looked from me to her and back at me. "If you don't want visitors today…" she began.

"No," I cut her off, "This one's always welcome."

She scowled at Stacey and told her, "Go easy. He's not doing too well today. His doctor will be here shortly. When she comes, I think it will be best that you leave." With that, she left.

"Whatsa matter with your girlfriend today?" Stacey asked.

I smiled. Stacey always managed to make me smile. "Sit down,"

I told her. "I'm glad you're here. I need to talk to you."

Stacey could see the seriousness of my mood. She sat and watched me closely. Her hands started to shake and she began bouncing her right leg, something I notice she does whenever she's excited or upset. I decided to get straight to business.

"My time is winding down," I told her. I didn't say any more than that. I wanted her to digest that bit first.

She didn't answer. She was quiet and she sat very still. She'd heard me loud and clear. I decided to continue.

"Don't worry. I'm ready to go. I've handled my affairs as best I could. I've made my peace with God. Outside of seeing my wife again, I'm ready."

Tears flooded Stacey's eyes. I handed her the box of tissue on my nightstand. I needed to say everything I wanted her to hear quickly before I broke down and cried too. There weren't enough tissues in the box for the both of us.

"I want to thank you for all you've done for me. Ever since the day you met me, you've hovered over me and protected me. You've sheltered me from my own negativity. You've been a ray of sunshine on most of my cloudy days. I couldn't have gotten through this final stage of my life without you. God sent me an angel to help escort me home, to help me to transition into a whole new world. You're beautiful. I'm sorry we didn't meet earlier and under different circumstances. You would have definitely tamed the beast in me. You're a good girl, a beautiful young woman. I wish you well. I wish you much luck in life and a whole lot of love. You have humbled this forty three year old man and made him realize what matters in life. I'll never understand why you chose me to waste all of your free hours on," I teased, "but I'm glad you did. I'm very fond of you. You've been the daughter I never had. Thank you for filling the gaps in my life with joy, peace, and laughter. Your family must be proud of you, especially your daddy. Are you a daddy's girl?"

Stacey grinned briefly, then cried aloud. She buried her head in her hands to muffle the sound. I stroked her mane. She looked up at me and wiped her eyes.

"My daddy's dead," she told me. "Died of cancer seven years ago. I didn't know he had it. He never appeared sick to me. I had no idea, and I didn't get to say goodbye. He was stubborn and selfish and you remind me of him." She cried some more. "I'm sorry," she blubbered. "I didn't mean to snap at you that way. I'm going to miss you. I've become very fond of you. I knew you were…*leaving*, but I guess I never really prepared myself. I guess I thought you would somehow get well one day, get out of that bed, leave this place, and be my daddy. I know it sounds crazy, but that's what I thought. That's what I wanted. I don't want you to go. Don't tell me it's almost time."

She laid her head on my chest. I rubbed her back and started to sing. Although I was way out of tune, I sang the few lines I could remember from CeCe Winans', "Don't Cry For Me."

> *Don't cry for me,*
> *Don't shed a tear.*
> *The time I had with you will always be.*
> *And when I'm gone, Please*
> *carry on. Don't cry for me.*

Stacey stayed with me until close to noon. She didn't want Dr. Kaylor to find her in my room in a mournful state. That would quite possibly damage her internship. When it was time to go, Stacey was in terrible shape. Her eyes were red and puffy and her usual bubbly nature was well hidden. She appeared lifeless and strained.

"Want me to come back later?" she asked almost inaudibly.

"No, not today." I told her while forcing back tears. She'd been through enough with me for today. We both needed time to get ahold of ourselves. She nodded her head and slowly turned to leave.

"Wait," I called out to her. "I almost forgot. I have something for you."

I reached down on the floor and picked up the plastic bag near my bed.

"Here," I told her. "This is for you. I handed her a bag of items I'd been collecting from the hospitality cart, things I thought she'd like. Stuffed animals, books, pens, cards, and perfume samples. I had also written her a poem, but I didn't want her to find that until she got home, so I didn't mention it.

"I wish I had something more to give," I told her, "but this is all I can manage considering…well…"

She looked inside the bag and smiled. Then, she kissed me on the forehead. More tears fell. She headed towards the door and left without looking back. Just as promised, Doc Kaylor showed up promptly at noon.

"Hello, Mr. Rutherford," she said and smiled. "How have you been?"

She continued before I could answer. "I hear you're not doing too well."

"You heard wrong, Doc," I told her. "I'm doing better than I have in a long time. I've got my affairs in order, I've got great friends, I've got a fine doctor, God's smiling upon me. I'm doing alright. I'm on my way to a better place, Doc. Heading to a place where I'll be fine for the rest of my days. No more stomach pains, no more heartaches."

She knew just what I meant by the heartaches.

"You seem to have found peace. That's good. How's Christine handling all of this?" she asked.

I didn't answer.

"Charles." She said my name the way my mother used to whenever she caught me doing something wrong. "Don't tell me Christine still doesn't know."

Again, I didn't answer.

"For God's sake, Charles. I've known you and Christine for years now. I don't know what's been going on with the two of you lately, but I know that Christine would be devastated to find out about your…about…well, you should have told her by now, don't you think? What are you doing? Are you trying to punish her for something?"

Suddenly, Doc wasn't just my doctor anymore. She was my friend and she was worried about me. I reached for her hand.

"You've been a good doctor and a better friend. I've always been able to count on you and I've always trusted you. You've got to trust me this time. I know what I'm doing. Let it be. Everything's alright," I told her.

She hung her head and paced a bit. I could tell she wasn't convinced. She was worried about Christine. I was too.

Doc and Christine went to college together. Doc was Christine's roommate for a couple of months until her parents came up with enough money for her to move out on her own. Doc and Christine lost touch until Chris started to experience some female issues. She found Doc's name listed in the yellow pages and decided to pay her old roommate a visit. Christine was pleased with her treatment and felt comfortable with Dr. Kaylor. Since I didn't have a general practitioner of my own, I adopted Doc Kaylor as well. I found her very attentive and very professional. She is a woman who sincerely cares about not only the physical, but also the emotional welfare of others. She was especially showing that trait today.

Doc spent almost thirty minutes with me checking my pulse, my blood pressure, and pressing on my stomach. She gave me a couple of painkillers and instructed me to get plenty of rest.

"Try not to move around too much," she told me. "Take it easy, Charles. Don't provoke the pain."

I nodded. Upon leaving, Doc gave me almost the same look Stacey had. I knew what it meant. I waved goodbye and smiled.

Chapter 14 - Christine

I was lying awake in bed, thinking about Conrad. This was becoming a norm for me. I went to bed thinking of him at night, and I woke up thinking of him as soon as I opened my eyes in the morning. I was in love.

I rolled over and looked at the clock. It was 7:59a.m. I decided to lie in bed for a couple of minutes more. I turned on my side and hugged my pillow. I closed my eyes and sighed. I could still smell traces of Conrad's Polo. I dug my nose deeper into the pillow and inhaled the scent.

No more than two minutes passed when I heard a banging on the kitchen door downstairs. The banging startled me. I rushed downstairs and looked out the kitchen window. I thought it might be Conrad, but the car parked outside in my driveway was not his. I became nervous. I stood quietly for a minute to listen for clues as to who was outside. The banging continued. I peeked out the door and saw a woman. I couldn't make out who it was, so I left the security latch on the door and opened it just a crack. It was Stacey.

"What are you doing here?" I asked her, confused and angry about her trying to beat my door down.

"Let me in," she demanded.

I yawned, and again I asked, "What are you doing here? What do you want?"

I could tell she was on a rampage, and I was sure it had something to do with Conrad. I wasn't up for any nonsense so early in the morning, so I tried to politely dismiss her.

"Look, Stacey, can you come back a little later. I'm barely awake and I've got..."

She cut me off.

"This can't wait. You need to let me in. I'm not leaving until you do," she insisted.

I could tell she was serious and I was still groggy and too tired to fight. I took the latch off the door and hesitantly let her in.

She stomped inside and eyed the house. Her eyes wandered from corner to corner.

"Is there something I could help you with?" I sarcastically asked her.

"You need to get dressed and come with me," she said.

"Excuse me?" I answered as I tipped my ear to make sure that I heard her right this time.

She repeated herself. "You need to come with me."

I laughed. "Oh, I do, do I? And tell me, where exactly is it that I need to go with you? If it's to see your Uncle Conrad, I manage that just fine from right here." I snickered. Stacey looked like she wanted to tear me apart. I shot her a "Don't-forget-I'm-the-woman-of-this-house," look and she quickly composed herself.

"Look," she said pleadingly. "I can't tell you just yet where I'm taking you, but it's a place you need to go. There's someone you need to see. Someone who really needs to see you."

She had my curiosity piqued. I questioned her further, but she insisted upon keeping the *who* and the *where* of her mission a secret. A part of me was afraid to go anywhere with her, but a larger part of me needed to have my curiosity satisfied. I instructed her to have a seat in the living room while I ran upstairs to wash up and dress.

I was done in minutes. I snatched up my purse and my keys and told little Miss Audacity I was ready to go.

"I'm going with you," I told her, "but on the condition that I drive. I don't know where you're taking me or who you're taking me to. I'm not going anywhere with you blind folded unless I'm going in my own car."

She rolled her eyes and sighed out loud.

"Look, Chris…Mrs. Rutherford. We have to do this my way.

Besides, like you said, you don't know where we're going and by the time we get there and are ready to head back, you probably won't have the energy to drive."

I was frightened now. The more I talked to Stacey, the more nervous she made me. I put my keys in my purse and looked at her suspiciously.

"Relax, Mrs. Rutherford. I'm not here to hurt you. Believe it or not, what I'm doing right now I'm doing to help you. Please don't ask too many questions during our ride. You'll find out everything you need to know in due time. Just hang tight and trust me. See if you can handle that," she said.

I locked up the house and followed Stacey to her car. I walked two paces behind her and mentally noted her license plate in case I would need it later. I checked my purse for my cell phone. It was there. 9-1-1 was only a three-button dial away.

"Buckle up," she warned. "I drive pretty fast."

She wasn't lying. Stacey headed down Main Street like a maniac. She whizzed in and out of traffic and ignored red lights. I noted every turn she made. I wasn't sure where we were going, but I would be sure I knew my way back.

We ended up at Grand Valley Memorial. I was very confused now and terribly anxious. "Is Conrad here?" I asked her.

She rolled her eyes at me again. Without answering, she got out of the car and slammed the door shut. She came around to my side of the car and opened the door,

"Let's go," She demanded.

She stomped ahead of me without looking back. I had a hard time keeping up with her steps. We went into the elevator and she pressed the button that took us to the third floor, the Cancer Unit. I furrowed my brow. This was becoming scarier by the moment. Stacey went to the nurse's station. I saw a look of familiarity on their faces.

"Is he awake yet?" she asked the nurse who didn't question the *he* Stacey was referring to.

"He's been in and out since early this morning," The nurse told her. "Go on in though. I'm sure he won't mind."

We went to the patient's room. Stacey opened the door slowly, peeking inside before letting me in. She turned to me and said, "He seems to be sleeping. Be quiet. Don't startle him."

We went inside. There was a man lying in the bed. He was turned away from us so I couldn't see his face. He was apparently an older man. His hair was graying and he had a slight wheezing and a raspy cough. Stacey motioned for me to sit down while she went over to the bed and stroked the man's head. He shifted and looked up at her. He took her by the hand.

"Hey you," he said weakly.

"Somebody's here to see you," she told him. "I know you'll probably be upset with me for doing this, but I've brought Christine here. You said you had everything in order except for her. I wanted to make sure that you had the chance to resolve every aspect of your life. Please forgive me for taking matters into my own hands, but know that I've done this for you."

Chapter 15 – Charles

I could hear the conversation between Stacey and Christine, and as much as I wanted to join in and to have my say, I was immobilized. I couldn't move. I couldn't speak. I couldn't open my eyes. I just lay there and consorted with death.

Christine poured out her heart to me last night. She confessed all of her sins to my lifeless body and my seemingly deaf ears. Her tears washed my face. She held my hand the entire time, and I tried to give here a squeeze to let her know I'd heard, but no matter how hard I tried, I couldn't manage to move a muscle.

I wanted to ease Christine's mind and to let her know that I forgave her, but I guess her peace would have to come from someone with more jurisdiction over her sins than me.

I felt my tense muscles relax. My mind was at ease and my stomach pains were suddenly no more. The bright light before me was calling my name and I was finally ready to head towards it. I was ready to find peace and contentment on the other side. I knew Christine would be fine. I made preparations for her that I was certain would be handled well on my behalf. Everything was in order. I was tired. It was time for me to surrender. I mentally let go of Christine's hand and placed mine in the hand of the leader of the band of angels that had come for me. We drifted off into the light in slow motion. As we did, I looked back. Christine was awake now and still holding my hand. She was talking to me, but I couldn't hear what she was saying. She felt my head and kissed my cheek. Then, she started to cry. I saw her press the button near my bed and call for the nurse. The nurse answered right away. Several doctors followed behind her. They checked the life monitor and found I was no longer with them. Christine balled up and wailed.

A nurse tried to lead her out of my room, but she refused to go.

"Don't cry, Christine. Don't cry for me." I tried to tell her. She couldn't hear me.

She clutched onto the chair near my bed and slid down the wall. She sat on the floor and helplessly watched as the doctors and nurses removed my body from the room. They wheeled me out. One of the nurses stayed behind and comforted Christine.

My band of angels did the same for me. They turned my attention from Christine and instructed me now to focus on the light. The journey was a long, but pleasant one. I thanked God the whole time that I had made my peace with him and for allowing me to join him soon. I thought of Stacey and prayed for guidance and protection over her. I thought of the reverend and was pleased that I felt no resentment towards him. I thought of my dad, grandma, and my brother, and tried let them know I was on my way. With a final glance at my weeping widow, I closed my eyes and trusted the band of angels to guide me home.

Chapter 16 – Christine

I held his hand while he slept. It felt just as good as it did when we used to curl up together in bed at night. I felt the intimacy between us return. Charles was my husband again. I was his wife. Everything that had gone wrong between us became no more than a memory. All that mattered was that we were together again and in love.

It must have been around two or three in the morning when it happened. All night, I drifted in and out of consciousness. I would wake periodically and watch Charles sleep. With my head on his shoulder and his hand still in mine, I felt a stinging sensation. Charles's hand was cold and numb. I didn't open my eyes. I just lay there, still holding on, telling myself it was a dream and that reality would set back in real soon. My body went numb and my eyes stayed shut. I didn't want to see with my eyes what my heart was telling me. I didn't want to see what I knew to be true.

Charles had left me. Just as the Bible promises, Death came like a thief in the night and stole Charles away from me. I wanted to cry, but the tears wouldn't fall. I lay still and consciously pictured myself with my husband at different stages of our relationship. I thought of our first meeting. I thought of how shy and demure I was and of how Charles broke through all of my barriers and swept me off my feet. I thought of our first date, and I remembered the tiniest details, like the huge spaghetti stain that ruined the lavender dress I had specially selected for the date because it modestly, but eye-catchingly showed my figure. Charles knew I was embarrassed and upset. Within minutes, he "accidentally" spilled pasta sauce on his white Oxford shirt.

The next day, I received a gift in the mail. Charles had purchased an identical lavender dress for me. He even got the size right. He informed me later that he had snuck a peek at the label while we danced. That's when I decided Charles was the kind of man I could love for the rest of my life.

I thought of all the trips Charles and I had taken together, the parties we hosted, the corny TV shows we pretended to enjoy watching together while we curled up on the sofa. I thought about our wedding day. It was beautiful and I was the happiest woman alive.

Those thoughts soothed me to sleep. I was no longer in control of my memories. My mind took over and played a slide show of my life with Charles in my head. Scene after scene flashed before me. Each picture was pleasant and comforting. It's true. The mind truly does have a way of protecting the heart.

I woke just a couple of minutes after seven. I looked at my husband, lying there beside me. He was dead. Charles Rufus Rutherford, my husband had been called home. I suddenly remembered the part of my marriage vows that stated that Charles and I would love each other until death do us part. That statement was inaccurate. I will love Charles forever. I wanted to tell him that. I should have told him last night. There's a lot I should have told Charles.

Thoughts of all the time that was wasted between Charles and myself took over and led me on a roller coaster of emotions. I was angry with Charles for excluding me from his life during his most critical moments. I was mad at myself for not investigating further and noticing that my husband needed me. I felt guilty and ashamed over having gotten involved with Conrad. I felt saddened that my life with Charles was over. I felt cheated by God who didn't reveal to me that my husband needed me. He never answered my prayer for a revelation, for guidance, and for patience. I felt nervous about my future. I had no idea what my next move was supposed to be? Last week, I was asserting myself, becoming independent, maturing. This week, I'm scared and unsure.

I felt Charles face. It was cool. He looked at ease and that comforted me a little, but I couldn't help feeling sorry for myself. I tried to maintain my composure. I tried hard not to break down, but my emotions caused tears that could have sunk Noah's Ark. I felt a tightening in my chest. I was dizzy and hot. I thought I would faint. I whimpered. I cried. I howled. I screamed.

I told Charles I loved him, that I would miss him, that I needed him. He couldn't hear me. He was gone. I kissed my husband goodbye and pressed the button for the nurse. A part of me believed she could do something to revive him. She came in immediately. In minutes, there were several of them, trying to lead me from Charles's room, but I wouldn't go. I never wanted to leave him and I was angry with him for leaving me.

The doctors put Charles on a stretcher and wheeled him out of the room. For them, it was business as usual. I wanted to follow him, but my body wouldn't move. I just sat there helplessly and cried. One of the young nurses wrapped her arms around me. She looked at me sympathetically and asked if there was anyone she could call for me.

"Yeah," I told her. "Call God and tell him I'm mad as hell."

She held me tighter. I squeezed her too. I needed something to cling on to because I felt like I was falling into a never-ending hole. I closed my eyes and rested my head on the nurse's shoulder. I pictured her in my head. Her white uniform sprouted wings and her hat turned into a halo. I heard her tell me that everything would be all right…and I believed her.

Chapter 17 - Christine

"You up, sleepy head?" Stacey asked me. She was carrying a tray of breakfast.

"Yeah," I replied groggily. "A part of me is anyway." "How'd you sleep?" she wanted to know.

"I tossed and turned most of the night, but I managed a few winks in between. I feel a little disoriented. I miss Charles so much already." I told her. "Thanks for staying with me last night. It was a really kind gesture. I don't think I would have been brave enough to close my eyes if you weren't here."

"No problem," she said. "Charles asked me to."

Her response was like an alarm clock buzzing in my ear. "Charles asked you to?" I asked her.

"Yeah," she smiled. "Charles is taking care of you even from the great beyond. He made several arrangements for you. That control freak." She joked. "He left instructions for everyone on how to care for you. He loved you. He's always loved you. I know you two encountered a couple of rough spots, but Charles indisputably treasured you, Christine."

I couldn't believe my ears. I repeated the question one more time.

"Charles asked you to stay the night with me?"

"He asked me to stay with you for a couple of weeks. I have two weeks left before I have to return to school. Charles told me you'd need someone to help you to come to terms with his dying. He wanted to make sure you were able to deal well with all of this before leaving you on your own," she told me.

I shook my head. It was just like Charles to dictate to me and to try to control everything. I was grateful to him and appreciated his concern, but I was also very annoyed that he seemed to leave me no choice in the matter.

"And you agreed?" I asked Stacey. "Am I supposed to accept the plans you and Charles have made for me? What if it's my wish to grieve in peace? What if I wish to be alone at this time? What if I want to go somewhere to be alone? Then what? Has Charles instructed you to follow me? What if…" I stopped short. I could see that Stacey, who had appeared tough as nails, was hurt by my response.

"You're right," she answered almost in a whisper. "Charles just wanted to make sure you didn't sit around brooding over him. He wanted to make sure you were able to adjust. I'm not here to invade your space. I'm here to help. Charles was sure you would need me. I promised him I wouldn't leave you. I assured him I would stay and help you to get on your feet. I don't want to break my promise to him, but I also don't want to be a nuisance to you. I can understand your needing space and privacy. I told Charles I was sure you'd want to be alone, but he insisted and he made me promise to stay."

I shook my head and smiled.

"I'm sorry," I apologized. "I sound so ungrateful. I really am glad you're here. Although I hate to admit it, I do need you. I wouldn't know what to do with myself if I were left alone right now. Charles was right. My controlling husband always did know best"

"If you want," Stacey said, "I'll leave. In this case, you're the one who knows what's best for you. You know what you want, what you need."

"No," I quickly responded. "I can't have you breaking a promise to Charles now, can I?"

I winked at Stacy. She smiled an awkward smile.

"Well," she said, "Since you're fully awake now, I might as well clue you in to the rest of the list."

I felt my brow furrow. "There's more?"

"Yup," she smiled, "There's more."

She pulled Charles list from her pocket and scanned his instructions. "I'm not supposed to let you sleep too late. Charles said you have a tendency to sleep away your troubles. He wants you up and moving around. He's given us a chore to complete today. He wants us to pack all of his belongings. Tomorrow, he wants us to donate them to charity. Charles doesn't want you hanging on to physical memories of him. He wants you to start your new journey through life as soon as possible. He said it would be easier that way."

"Is that what the two of you did during your visits with him, write a manual on how to handle fragile Christine?" I snapped.

Stacey didn't say anything, but rather looked at me with genuine concern.

I managed a faux smile. "So he wants me to box him up, huh? Do I get to keep anything at all?" I didn't wait for an answer. "Hmm." I laughed out loud. Stacey looked nervous. I let her in on the joke. "The funny thing is, Stacey, if you look around, you'll see that I've already put everything that belongs to Charles in boxes. I packed him up a while ago." My tears started to fall uncontrollably. "I thought he'd left me. I thought he had defiled out marriage and I didn't want anything more to do with him. Box him up, huh?"

I looked up at the ceiling, "Well, Charles, Honey, that's already been done," I told him.

Guilt caused my chest to clamp up and my head to ache. I cried some more. Stacey patiently sat with me until I grew tired and stopped. She fidgeted and played with a couple of small holes in the quilt on the bed. The quilt belonged to Charles. His grandmother made it. I didn't tell her that. I instantly made up my mind that even if that quilt ended up looking like Swiss cheese, it would stay on my bed forever.

"What's the next item on the list? For you to hand me a tissue, dry my tears and wipe my runny nose?" I sarcastically asked Stacey. I couldn't help taking stabs at her. A part of me was grateful for her assistance, but another part of me hates her. I hate her for being the one who spent most of Charles's last days with him, comforting him, making him smile, being his crutch. And now, here she is, playing the woman of the house and treating me like a child at Charles's request, telling me what to do and how and when to do it all. I hate her for being by my husband's side during the most critical stage of his life and doing the job that should have been mine. I hate her now for continuing to take on a role that belongs to me.

Stacey smirked. "Look, Christine. I think you could do with some time alone. The next couple of items on the list involve going downtown. If you show me the boxes of Charles belongings, I'll take them for you."

"They're in the garage," I told her. "There's a box marked PICTURES. I want that one. If you don't mind, and if you can manage it, I'd like to have that box brought back into the house. I need to put the pictures back where they belong.

"You got it," she said and winked. "I'll be gone for just about two hours. Will you be alright?" I nodded. "Need anything while I'm out?"

"Probably groceries." I answered.

"That's on the list," she responded and laughed. I laughed too. "My goodness," I said. "Well then, get my purse.

You'll need a cheque."

"She pulled a couple of bills out of her pocket. Covered," she said and laughed again. "Christine, the man loved you and as you can see, he had plenty of time to think of how to prove it to you.

You're a lucky woman. We don't all find such good men."

Tears flowed freely from my eyes. Stacey took that as her cue to leave.

"Two hours," she yelled back from the staircase. "I shouldn't be much longer than that. I left my cell phone number on the nightstand in case you need me."

I heard Stacey leave. I was alone in the house for the first time since Charles died. Although I had been alone in the house many times before, this time it seemed extra quiet and I felt extra lonely. I hugged the pillow on Charles's side and slept.

Chapter 18 - Christine

The phone rang and woke me from a deep sleep. I checked the caller ID. It was Conrad. It's amazing how easily I've managed to remove him from both my mind and my heart. I hesitated in answering. I wasn't sure if I was ready to talk to him. I decided to pick up.

"Hello," I said in a daring tone.

"Chris," he answered, "How are you doing? Are you alright?

I've been worried about you, but I wanted to give you a little space."

"I'm just fine, Reverend," I answered angrily.

I could tell he sensed my mood and that he picked up on the deliberately formal address.

"I could come over if you need me to, Chris. I don't have anything on my agenda for today. I left it open for you," he said sweetly.

"I'm busy," I coldly replied.

"Anything I can help you with?" he pressed.

"You can help me to come to terms with the fact that I'm an adulteress. And you can help me to understand why the man I thought I was falling in love with took part in deceiving me by keeping secrets," I told him. "That's what you can help me with."

He was silent for a moment, and then he began his defense. "Charles asked me not to say anything. He wanted to handle things his way, and I thought I owed him that. You know what else he asked of me, Chris? He asked me to continue to love you, to take care of you. He gave us his blessing." He said that in a tone that sounded too elated for my liking.

"Conrad, my husband was dying," I reminded him, "And you didn't keep his secret in an effort to honour his wishes. You kept his secret because you knew that my knowing about Charles's condition would have caused me to make every effort to fix my marriage. I would have tried desperately to right the wrongs. You knew that I wouldn't have belonged to you anymore, that whatever it was that we had would have been over instantly. I can't believe how selfish you've been. I can't believe how self-centered I've been. There will never be anything between us again, Conrad. Please just leave me alone. I need time to grieve. I'm suffering two losses."

He wasn't ready to give up. "I know you're going through a rough time right now, Christine, but we belong together. There was a connection forming between the two of us, a strong connection. I'll give you whatever time you need to get over Charles. If you'll allow me to, I'll be there, right by your side to comfort you while you find yourself again. Please, Christine, don't shut me out. I love you. I don't believe that our involvement was spontaneous and erratic. I believe that our involvement was spontaneous and erratic. I believe that our souls have been searching for each other for some time now. Charles's dying may have closed one door for you, but God always opens another. I know that a large part of you love me too."

"Don't blame God for what happened between us, Conrad," I retorted. "Nothing about our relationship was godly. We locked God out."

"Christine," he pleaded, "Our timing might have been all wrong, but what happened between us was right. I believe in destiny, Chris. I believe you are my destiny. I won't give up on us. I'll give you time and I'll give you space, but I won't give you up."

"Goodbye, Conrad," was the only answer I could give. With that, I hung up and went into the living room. I needed to take my husband out of the box I'd put him in.

I unpacked the pictures one by one and kissed each of them before restoring them to their original resting places. I talked to some of them, believing that if I did, somehow, Charles would hear me. Unpacking the pictures made me feel like Charles would be coming back home, like his death would prove just as premature as my packing him up.

I spent over two hours emptying the box. Remnants of Charles were all over the living room. He looked content. I was pleased.

Once I had the pictures arranged, I lit every candle in the living room and held a private vigil for my husband. The smell of vanilla permeated the room. I reclined my exhausted body on the sofa. I looked around at the pictures of Charles and remembered where and when each one was taken. I smiled at many of the memories as tears took charge of my eyes. My eyelids suddenly felt heavy and I needed to sleep.

As soon as I closed my eyes, someone impatiently knocked on the door. I became nervous at first, but grew more annoyed with each bang. I flung the door open and prepared myself to engage in verbal combat. Instead, I softened at the sight of the large bouquet of flowers that greeted me.

"Are you Christine Rutherford?" asked the young delivery driver?

"Yes," was all I muttered.

"Then these are for you." He handed me the flowers. "Sign here please," he said.

I signed for my first tangible piece of proof that my husband's death was a reality.

The driver's nod sealed the transaction. I took the flowers inside and laid them on the coffee table in the center of the living room. It was amazing how much the colourful bouquet decorated the area. I removed the card from its holder and read it.

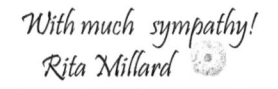

With much sympathy!
Rita Millard

"Rita Millard?" I thought hard about who Rita Millard might be. The name didn't ring any bells and for reasons I can't explain, that disturbed me. I hunted the phone book and look down the listing of Millards. There weren't many, and none of them were Ritas. Since there were only a few names listed, I decided to make some calls. I started from the top of the list and worked my way down.

Each time I asked for Rita, I was informed that I had dialed the wrong number. Some people are good with remembering names, others at remembering faces. Usually, I am good at both. Rita Millard was breaking my track record. I believe the reason I can't let Rita Millard's name to rest in my mind is because a part of me is still not convinced that Charles wasn't cheating on me during the last part of our marriage. Maybe guilt has got me paranoid.

I began tending to minor chores around the house and pretended that Rita Millard's name was no longer on my mind. In the middle of doing laundry, I heard a loud knock at the door. This time, curiosity caused me to dash to open it. Wishful thinking told me it was Rita Millard coming to send her condolences in person.

It was Conrad.

"Hi," he said timidly. "I'm busy, Reverend," was my cold response. I stressed *Reverend*, and instantly turned the visit into a formal one. Conrad looked to the ground. I felt guilty. It's nothing quite like witnessing a cheerless man. "Come in," I told him, "but just for a minute."

He perked up a little.

"How have you been, Christine," he asked. "Fine," was all I offered.

I led the way to the living room where we sat for a couple of minutes in an uncomfortable silence. Finally, I broke it.

"Conrad," I could tell I was taking him on a roller coaster ride, referring to him formally, then informally. It seemed one minute I considered him my friend and wanted to keep him close, then the very next, I wanted desperately to let him go and simply make him my pastor again, my superior. I wanted to forget that he and I had taken our relationship to another level. I wanted to somehow erase the past and start it all over again.

"Why exactly is it that you're here?" I asked him, "What is it you want from me? I can't offer you anything. I shouldn't have offered you what I did. Things should never have changed between us. How did we let it happen? How did I manage to step so far out of character that I hardly even know myself anymore? What is even more perplexing to me is how you, my mentor, confident, and friend, not only stood by and watched as I stepped out of character, but enabled me, encouraged me even. At a time when you should have forced me to step back and to reevaluate my feelings, my thoughts, and my actions, you took advantage of me."

"Is that how you feel, Chris?" he asked me. "Like I took advantage of you?"

"Yes, Conrad, if the truth be told, that's how I feel. I believe you have taken advantage of me. Maybe I'm putting too much of the blame on you. Maybe I'm using you to lessen the guilt I feel, but for now, that's my reality. The truth as I see it tells me that I have been very wrong in my doings, and that my marriage has failed mainly because of my own misconduct, but I also feel that you enabled it to dissipate and I believe that you took full advantage of me. That's why it hurts me to be in your presence. Looking at you intensifies the guilt I feel. I can't stand to be around you right now. This is the worst time for you to invade my space. Please, Conrad, respect my privacy. Become my reverend again.

Don't focus on being anything more to me."

Conrad held his head and I saw a tear fall. I felt miserable, and I felt that I had set him up for a fall. My life seemed to be both spinning out of control and resolving itself at the same time. I was confused and I felt lost. I lacked confidence in my ability to make good decisions for myself. Maybe Charles knew me better than I gave him credit for. His making lists and sorting things out for me was probably the best parting gift he could have given me. Conrad spent the next couple of minutes telling me how much he cared for me and of how he wished we were in a better place in life. Even though he still believes that he and I are destined to be together, he has agreed to respect the fact that I need space. I said nothing and allowed him to fully vent. As soon as he was done, I speechlessly smiled my thanks and escorted him to the door. We parted with a quick one-handed hug.

I closed the door and watched him from the window. Stacey drove up just as Conrad prepared to get into his car. I saw Stacey hug him and rub his head. They chatted for a minute before parting. I quickly backed away from the window and made myself comfortable in the living room. Stacey walked in and called my name. Before I could emerge from the living room, I heard her trudging up the stairs. She retraced her steps.

"Oh, there you are," she said while looking at me suspiciously. I knew exactly what she was thinking. "I caught Revvy as he was leaving."

I answered her unspoken request for clarification. "Yeah, he stopped by to see how I was making out. I told him that I was managing fine and that he shouldn't worry about me. I told him the only thing I need from him right now is space."

Stacey smiled. "Hmm," was the way she answered. "I put the groceries on the counter," she informed me. "We won't need any of them tonight though," she told me. "We're going out to eat. My treat. I won't be with you much longer. Tomorrow night's the viewing and the funeral's the next. I'll have to leave to head back to Philly soon after that. I want to do something special with you before I go."

I nodded and ran upstairs. I closed my bedroom door and cried for two reasons. First, because Stacey's sweetness was touching, and second, because she'd reminded me that soon, I'd be putting Charles in his grave, burying him in the dirt from whence he came.

Chapter 19 - Christine

Dinner was delectable. Stacey took me to a seafood restaurant simply called Captain's. I'd never been there before. The atmosphere was just what I needed to clear my mind and to relax. The place was decorated with palm trees and the sound of seagulls and the ocean soothed and comforted me. The waiters wore cute Bermuda shorts and a calypso band played softly at intervals. I felt like I had gone on a mini vacation, like I'd escaped my world and journeyed into another.

I kicked my shoes off as soon as I made my way into the house. All I needed to complete my night now was a warm bath and some good uninterrupted sleep. Nytol would help me with that.

First, I decided to check the caller ID. I was sure someone would be calling for more information on Charles's viewing, funeral time, or to express condolences. I quickly searched through the nine entrees and made mental note to return calls. One of the entries was from a "private caller". I hated those. I dialed my voice mailbox to see if the caller left a message. There wasn't one. Rita Millard came to mind, but I decided not to ruin my night with speculative thoughts of her.

I ran upstairs, found my half empty box of Calgon, and filled the tub with warm water. Stacey was in the guest bedroom adjacent the bathroom. She must have worn herself out today because I could already hear her snoring.

I laid my head on my bath pillow and soaked for almost an hour. Thoughts of Charles took over my mind. I remembered every fond moment he and I had ever shared and tears fell. I missed him so much already. I had so many regrets, but I tried to think positively. I told myself that Charles knew I loved him and I spent the remainder of my night reminding myself that he loved me too.

Morning came quickly. Charles's viewing would be this afternoon at three o'clock. I'm not ready to see him lying cold and lifeless in a casket. I hope they've put his good suit on him. I sent two of his outfits to the morgue. I wasn't sure which would fit him best. He liked the navy one so much better than the black. I hope they trimmed his mustache. Charles would be upset to know that he was being looked upon by many while sporting a raggedy mustache. The man had his pride. Stacey had taken care of all of the details for today. She's such a Godsend and I will surely miss her. She'll be heading back to Philly sooner than I'd like.

I looked at the clock. It was already just after nine. I got out of bed, washed up, and dressed myself in the outfit I would wear to the viewing. I knew that as time passed, I would lose the strength to do much of anything. I went down the hall and peeked into Stacey's room. Her curtains were drawn and her bed was made. She was already downstairs.

As I headed down, I smelled bacon. I love bacon, but today, I have no appetite for it.

"Hey there, Sleepy," Stacey said with bright eyes and a wide smile. "You're up just in time for breakfast. I was sure I would have to pack yours on a plate and reheat it later. Now, you can join me."

"I'm not hungry," I told her. She looked disturbed by that. I wasn't sure if it was because she was worried about me or because she'd gone through great lengths to fix such an enjoyable breakfast. I decided to sit and nibble on a little something as a way of thanking Stacey for her effort. Nibbling turned into devouring. I was hungrier than I thought.

"You gonna be alright today?" Stacey asked me as we ate. "Not sure." I needed to be honest.

"I'll be right there with you. Today and tomorrow will be hard for you. For us both, but everything will be alright from then on. You'll see. And even though I'll be back in Philly, don't think I'm can't be there for you. As a matter of fact, I'm expecting you to keep in touch. I'll be real hurt if you don't."

I smiled. I couldn't say too much, but Stacey read me well. We finished breakfast in silence. I insisted upon cleaning up. I needed to keep myself busy.

Stacey went upstairs to dress. While I was cleaning, Lydia called with last minute questions regarding Charles's funeral. He'd put her in charge. More flowers were delivered to the house and phone calls continued pouring in. I felt loved, but also suffocated. I decided to take a long drive in the country. I didn't tell Stacey because I knew she'd insist upon coming along. Instead, I left her a note in a very visible place.

The warm breeze felt good on my face. I turned on the radio and sang along with each of the songs that came on, rewriting quite a few lyrics. Usually, I exceed the speed limit. Today, my drive was leisurely and deliberate, the way the remainder of my life would be.

During the drive, I talked to Charles. I knew he could hear me. I told him of how I was feeling, of my plans for the future. I thanked him for handling things for Stacey and me. I asked him to help me to deal with life without him. I told him to give me signs to help me to make wise decisions.

Finally, I told him I loved him and that I was sure I'd be seeing him again someday. I cried a few tears, and I smiled a little. I drove for hours. I drove until it was almost time to see my husband. I thought about the viewing and mustered inner strength. Once I was able to pick myself up, I headed home to pick up Stacey.

I honked the horn to let Stacey know I was back. She was dressed and ready to go. Her eyes were red and puffy. I could tell she made constructive use of her time alone also. I hadn't thought about it, but Stacey and Charles had become close, and she too, needed time to grieve.

She got into the car without saying a word. I reached for her hand and squeezed it. I winked at her, letting her know we'd both be alright. She got into the car without saying a word. I winked at her, letting her know we'd both be alright. She smiled through the remainder of her tears that needed to fall. We drove to the viewing in silence.

We wanted to be the first ones at the church, but when we got there, a whole committee of mourners surprisingly greeted us. They wore dark clothing and looked dismal, but each of them wore plastered smiles. I figured this must be another piece of Charles's plan. A young man I didn't recognize met me at the entrance of the churchyard and insisted upon valet parking the car. Stacey and I were a little confused, but we decided to oblige him.

A couple of ushers greeted us as we entered the church and led us to our seats in the front row. I had planned on greeting people and maybe making a short unrehearsed speech, but I guess Charles had something else in mind. I liked his plan better. Everyone was seated by the time Stacey and I walked in. Lydia Bohler was at the front acting as the hostess. She hugged me and whispered her condolences in my ear. I noticed that Charles's casket was closed. I grew nervous. My hands started to shake and my knees buckled. Daniel Peters, a member of the Deacon Board caught me before I fell to the ground.

"Where's my husband?" I asked him.

"He's here," he told me. "Please, don't worry yourself. Everything's alright. Lydia's got everything under control. Take your seat. You need to relax." He held onto me until I was securely seated. Stacey sat in the chair next to me and held my hand. I felt like I was going to burst into tears, but I held them back and silently prayed for strength.

Once everyone was seated, Lydia began speaking. What I thought would be a very informal viewing turned into a formal service. Lydia welcomed everyone and opened the viewing in prayer. She prayed for me, and for everyone who loved Charles. Then, she read a poem by Nikki Giovanni called "Weep Not." I was touched. Lydia then called Shelly-Anne, her daughter to the podium. Shelly-Anne sang "Don't Cry for Me" by CeCe Winans. I smiled. That was definitely a request made by Charles. My husband loved CeCe. Shelly-Anne sang so beautifully that I had no choice but to cry. Stubborn tears wouldn't let me be.

When Shelly-Anne was done with her song, several of Charles's close friends stepped up to the podium one by one and said some kind words about him. Each one either shook my hand or hugged me on the way up. I was surprised to see some of Charles's old college buddies and people he worked with long ago that I was sure he had lost touch with. There were a few people there that I didn't recognize, but I assumed Charles met them somewhere during his journey through life.

Lydia returned to the podium and announced that she would be opening the casket soon. She didn't want to open it while everyone was in the room, so she instructed everyone, including me, to go into the next room where hors d'oeuvres were being served.

I was led to the front of the feeding line, and then escorted back to the room where my husband's body lay. Lydia stood by the casket, guarding it. Next to Lydia was a huge portrait of Charles on an easel. The instructions above the easel urged people to inscribe their condolences. I looked at Lydia and smiled. Then, I looked down at Charles and did the same. I leaned over and kissed his cheek. Then, I whispered in his ear, "I love you." I stroked his cheek and massaged his neatly trimmed mustache. I felt the collar of his navy suit, and smiled at the perfect way it fit. Charles looked handsome and peaceful. I knew he was alright and that I would be too. I hugged Lydia and thanked her for everything. She squeezed me tight. She informed me that Charles requested that his casket be closed tomorrow at the funeral.

"He thought it would be easier that way," she told me. "He wants us to mourn him today, and celebrate him tomorrow."

"He does, does he?" I answered as I looked at Charles and shook my head. "You're some man, Charlie Rutherford," I told him.

At that time, others emerged from the back and paid Charles their last respects. The service went beautifully. It wasn't nearly as bad as I had anticipated. I felt comforted and loved.

Stacey and I waited around until everyone left. Lydia stuck around and made sure that everything was put back in its place. Before closing up the church, Lydia offered to take Charles's picture to the car. It had been filled with messages of love. It was beautiful and would be treasured. I knew exactly where I would hang it.

Stacey and I talked about the viewing. We agreed that if the funeral tomorrow is as beautifully planned, we could definitely handle it just as well. Almost simultaneously, we sighed with satisfaction.

When we got home, we had some herbal

tea and actually watched a show. We chose *Everybody Loves Raymond* because we needed to laugh. Stacey went upstairs after the show was over. She needed to finish packing. I remained in the living room and decided to read some of the comments people had written on Charles's picture. Some of the messages were humourous, some sad, others sentimental. Quite a few began with "I'll never forget the time when…". I wonder if Charles realized how many lives he enhanced and how many special memories he helped to create. I continued to read. My hands shook and my heart tightened as I
read one of the messages:

"You may be gone, but surely not forgotten. I still see you everyday in a way I wish you could have seen yourself." Love, Rita

I was more curious now than ever as to who Rita was. I took my mind on a journey through tonight's service. I though about every face I came across from the time I entered the church until the time I left, trying to figure out which person was Rita. Of the people I saw that I didn't recognize, I wouldn't expect any of them to be. Something tells me Rita is young and beautiful, someone like Stacey, maybe a fraction older. I don't remember seeing anyone I didn't know that fit that description. It upsets me that I have no idea who this mystery woman is that says she still sees my husband everyday in a way she wishes he could see himself. What does that mean? I suddenly felt infuriated by a woman I didn't even know. I hated her for making me feel uneasy and suspicious about my husband at a time when I shouldn't feel anything but love for him.

I put the picture on the coffee table face down. I snatched up the remote and changed the channel. I couldn't sleep, so I decided to let the TV baby-sit me. I wasn't in an Everybody Loves Raymond type of mood anymore, so I flipped until I came upon a show that reflected how I was feeling on the inside. I caught a Rocky marathon.

Chapter 20 – Christine

When Stacey came downstairs in the morning, she found me draped over the sofa half awake with the TV still on.

"Did you fall asleep down here?" she asked.

"Guess I did," I told her as I rubbed my eyes to focus in on her better.

"You couldn't have been too comfortable," she said.

"As comfortable as I would have been in my bed," I snapped back.

Stacey raised her eyebrows at my mood.

"You seemed fine last night? Are you upset about today? You didn't stay up all night thinking about the funeral did you?" she wanted to know.

"No, that's not it." I told her, which unintentionally implied that there was something wrong.

"What's going on, Christine?" Stacey was concerned. I tried to think up a quick lie that wouldn't be too bad to tell. Then, I decided against it.

"You see the flowers on the table here?" I asked her. "Yeah," she answered suspiciously.

"They're from a woman named Rita Millard." Stacey looked confused. "Did Charles ever mention her to you?"

"No," was all Stacey said. I could tell she was eager to hear more.

"She's a mystery to me. When the flowers came, I was curious about her, but I dismissed my suspicions. Until last night, that is. Read her inscription on Charles's picture."

Stacey saw that the picture was face down. Her eyes questioned me about that. Mine gave her an answer. She hunted through the condolences until she found the one added by Rita Millard.

"Humph," she grunted after reading it. "I see what you mean.

And you have no idea who she is?"

"None," I told her.

Stacey looked as annoyed as I felt. A part of me appreciated that, and another part was concerned by it. I suddenly hated Stacey for the way she reacted to the idea of there being another woman in Charles's life. It was almost as though she felt cheated on too. I glared at her. She raised a brow. I turned my head.

Without formally excusing myself, I left Stacey standing in the living room alone and headed upstairs to wash up. I didn't feel like thinking about Rita What's Her Name anymore, and I didn't feel like looking at Stacey either. I needed to be alone.

I soaked in a warm bath until I felt aroma therapeutically healed. Stacey met me outside the bathroom door just as I was stepping out.

"Lydia Bohler called," she told me. "She said you should wear something bright and colourful. Something cheery."

"Humph," I grunted. "Another one of Charles's orders?" "I s'pose," she shrugged.

I hunted all through my closet for something bright and cheery to wear on the gloomiest day of my life. I found the perfect thing, a soft pink suit. I'd wear it with a white blouse and my pretty pink and mint green scarf.

Once I was dressed, I looked myself over. I was beautiful. My suit made me appear delicate, so I needed for my hair and makeup to make me look strong and in control. I put on just a tad bit of pink lipstick. Charles would be pleased. Heaven forbid I go to his funeral looking like I'm some kin to Jezebel. I smiled. I looked in the mirror and spoke to the picture of my husband taped to the corner.

"Well, Charles," I did a pirouette. "How do I look? Do you approve?"

Stacey called from downstairs. "Christine, it's almost time to go."

I smiled at Charles's picture. "I'll take that as a yes," I told him. I blew him a kiss and went downstairs. Stacey was waiting with the car keys in hand.

"You look nice," she told me.

She looked good too, and I told her so. She had on a baby blue pants suit. Her hair was pulled back into a neat bun. She looked younger, but very sophisticated. I reached for her hand. I wanted her to know I was sorry about earlier. She understood.

Stacey drove us to the church at a cruising rate of no more than forty miles per hour. That's really slow for Sister Lead Foot. Neither of us was in a hurry to bury Charles. It seemed too final, too much like an end.

When we arrived at the church, it was like déjà vu. The parking lot was full. The same valet that met us at the gate last night met us at the gate again today. A couple of women from the usher board greeted us at the entrance to the church. Instead of wearing their usual navy uniforms, they had on canary yellow suits. They led Stacey and me inside where we were both stunned by what we saw.

The dismal hall that sweet, but sorrowful last night was alive with laughter. Balloons were everywhere. People were standing around and socializing. There were soft drinks on a table in the corner of the room. Pictures of Charles and I were all over the room. They represented every stage of our relationship, our courtship, marriage, family, outings, dinner parties, and Charles's college years. People had decorated the room with their favourite photographic memory of Charles. I was overjoyed. I made my way around the room, looking at every picture. I laughed and cried at the same time. As I looked at the photos, people came to me and explained the pictures and reminded me of special times they shared with Charles. It was fantastic.

Once I had made my way around the room, Lydia called everyone to sit. She began Charles's funeral by saying a few words about her relationship with Charles. She then informed everyone of Charles's accomplishments in the church and of his volunteer work in the community. She spoke of him as a dedicated and loving husband and a great friend. Her daughter, Shelly-Anne and Damon, one of the younger ushers sang a song of celebration. It was very festive and fitting. Then, Stacey went to the podium and surprised me with a poem that Charles had written for me. She followed that poem with another that she wrote to Charles. Both were beautiful and very heartfelt.

Lydia then announced that some of Charles's college buddies, former co-workers and friends would give two-minute recollections of fun times they had with Charles. Each of them told funny and embarrassingly cute stories that I had never heard before. I laughed aloud. Charles's funeral was definitely unlike any I've even been to. I never expected to have so much fun at my husband's memorial service. I almost felt guilty, but I know that Charles would be disappointed that his plan to make me totally happy would have failed. It wasn't until now that I realized how much Charles loved me. All of this was being done for me, not him. I looked towards his closed casket and smiled.

Reverend Baxter emerged from the back of the hall and made his way to the podium. He looked at me uncomfortably as he closed the service with parting words to Charles and comforting words to me. He touched Charles's casket as he spoke. He referred to Charles as his dear friend and his brother. Then, the reverend made an announcement. He held up a silver plaque and read its inscription, *Charles Rutledge Auditorium*. Conrad had dedicated the newly remodeled church auditorium to Charles. I was moved. Conrad presented me with the plaque and announced that a formal ceremony would be held next Sunday afternoon to officially name and dedicate the auditorium.

Everyone applauded as Reverend Baxter reached for my hand. I took him in my arms instead. As I held him, I felt a cool and gentle breeze cross my cheek. I knew exactly what that was. Charles had kissed me goodbye.

Festive music started to play. Liturgical dancers emerged from the halls, wearing white and holding batons adorned with colourful strands of ribbon which they twirled as they celebrated. They danced to CeCe's song, *King of Kings*. Their routine was dazzling. I found myself stomping to the beat. Others clapped and sang along. Charles's funeral was not dismal at all. It was a festive home going party. Charles wanted the people he loved most to celebrate his going home to be with God. Charles had the right idea. The only tears that were shed today were happy ones.

I looked at Stacey.

"You take notes from today?" I asked her. "Sure did," she said.

"This is what I want when it's my time. You got that?" I smiled "Got it, babe," she said and winked.

Just as we did yesterday, Stacey and I stayed until everyone but Lydia had left. This time, Conrad stayed behind too. He went to the kitchen and helped Lydia to clean up. Stacey and I collected the photos off the wall. We sang *King of Kings* as we worked. I came across a picture that caused me to stop singing.

It was of a beautiful, young, black, woman. Something told me she must be Rita. I pulled the picture off the wall and checked the back of it. Just as I thought, there was an inscription, *In memory of my good friend. May you rest in peace, Rita.*

"What's the matter, Chris?" Stacey asked me.

"I just came across a picture of Rita Millard," I told her. "Here she is."

I showed her the photo. Stacey stared at it a moment, then read the message on the back. That jealous look crept across her face again.

"Who is she?" she wanted to know.

"I don't know who she is," I snapped.

Stacey ignored me and continued to pull pictures off the wall. "She was here," she informed me.

"Who," I asked her. "Rita?"

"Yeah," Stacey told me. "I saw that woman, or at least someone who looked very much like her. She sat across from us about two rows back. She had a young boy with her. He appeared to be around six or so."

She dug through her stack of pictures and handed one to me.

"This is the little boy right here."

I laughed. "No," I told her. "That's Charles when he was younger. I have some pictures from his earlier years at home. They're so cute. I'll have to show them to you when we get back."

Stacey looked confused. "I could have sworn this was the little boy. This looks just like him."

I turned the picture over. There was writing on the back. When I read it, my heart beat fast, my hands shook, and I could feel beads of sweat rolling off my face. Stacey sat me down in a chair while she mumbled something about the day's events being too much for me. I didn't answer. I handed her the picture with the inscription face up. She was just as stunned as I was when she read it.

I took the picture back from Stacey and examined it. The boy on the front looked just like my husband. No paternity test necessary. This child is Charles's son. Charles and I were married five years ago. We dated just short of a year. Rita was the woman before me, but for some reason, Charles never mentioned her. Throughout our years together, I had never heard the name Rita Millard, nor had I seen her picture. Rita Millard was Charles's best-kept secret.

A part of me wanted to hunt Rita Millard down. I had lots of questions to ask. Another part of me wanted to permanently remove thoughts of her from my mind.

Stacey finished collecting the pictures off the wall. Then, she gathered our things, informed Conrad and Lydia that we would be leaving, and quickly led me to the car. I felt dazed. Stacey drove us home in silence.

As soon as we made it inside the house, I ran upstairs to my bedroom. I lay across the bed and cried. All kinds of emotions took over, sadness, confusion, a sense of betrayal, jealousy, rage. I reached for my bottle of Nytol. I needed to sleep.

Chapter 21 – Christine

Between the Nytol and all that's happened in the past couple of weeks, I was cast into a deep sleep. I was barely awake when I felt Stacey shaking me roughly. She called my name over and over until I opened both of my eyes and focused on hers.

"You gotta wake up," she told me.

"Rita's here."

I didn't hear her at first, so I turned over and tried to drift back to sleep. She repeated herself.

"Christine, Rita Millard is here. She's downstairs. Wake up. Come on, get up." She sounded anxious. Hearing Rita Millard's name made me snap to attention. I sat straight up in the bed, placed my feet firmly on the ground, and focused on Stacey.

"Rita's here?" I questioned her.

"She's downstairs waiting to see you," Stacey told me. "Let's go to the bathroom and splash some water on your face."

I went with her, following slowly. The Nytol wasn't done working on me yet. I splashed water on my face then headed downstairs. Rita Millard was in my living room sipping tea. Seeing her face-to-face sobered me up. I couldn't believe it. Charles's mystery woman was right there in my living room. I looked her over completely, covering everything about her from head to toe. Her five-foot, seven-inch thin frame made me look overweight. Her neatly combed straight jet-black hair made my dyed black nappy dreads look like a used Brillo pad, and her perfectly painted face made me look old and plain. Her nails were French manicured. Mine were short and chewed, and her taut stomach made me appear to be five months with child. No wonder Charles hid her from me.

She moved forward and extended her hand. I left it suspended. "Hi," she said, "I'm Rita. Rita Millard. The flowers I sent you look beautiful in this room. I'm glad you saw fit to display them."

I didn't answer her. I continued to busy myself studying everything about her, the way she smelled, the way she walked, the way her voice sounded, etc. She was beautiful. I hated her.

"You had a son with my husband," was the way I chose to say hello. She grimaced and looked embarrassed.

"Yes," she answered, "I did. I gave birth to Charles's son seven years ago."

"Why don't I know you?" I asked her. "Why haven't I heard your name before or heard about the child? Had Charles seen him? Was he a part of his life? What did you mean by you still see him everyday in ways you wish he could see himself?"

I had many questions, and Rita Millard wouldn't be allowed to leave my home today until she gave me answers to all of them.

I could tell Rita was prepared. Stacey stood in the corner, gearing herself to be our referee. I wanted to be alone with Rita. Stacey had nothing to do with this. Charles was my husband, not hers. I dismissed her.

"Leave us alone, Stacey. Go and make sure you're all packed." I demanded.

"I'm done." Stacey told me.

I shot her a scowl that let her know she gave the wrong answer.

She quickly left the room.

"I know you have a lot of questions and I'm prepared to answer all of them," Rita told me. "That's why I'm here. I should have come a long time ago, when Charlie was…" She stopped short.

I hated her for mentioning my husband's name with such familiarity.

"What exactly was your relationship with Charlie?" I sarcastically mocked. "How old is your son? How long have you been involved with my husband?" I asked her.

By now, tears flooded my eyes, making her a five-foot, seven- inch blur. I sat and denied my knees a chance to buckle. Rita saw my discomfort and grew nervous. She began to fidget and invited herself to a spot on my sofa.

"Please, Mrs. Rutherford,"

I appreciated her acknowledging me as Charles's wife. I half grinned at the show of respect.

"I need to explain some things to you. My visit here is as difficult for me as it must be for you."

I "humphed" at her, letting her know I doubted that very much.

Nonetheless, she persisted. She showed

up at my door to tell me something, and she was determined to do it.

"I must start by clearing something up. I know that you and Charlie have been married for just over five years now. I met Charlie seven years ago." She informed me. I interrupted her prepared speech.

"My husband's name is Charles." Her familiarity with him was infuriating me.

"I'm sorry," she quickly corrected herself,

"Charles. How insensitive of me." She gave a friendly smile. I didn't give one back.

"Charles," she continued, "and I met seven years ago. We met at a place called LaNello's Restaurant. We were attending an engagement party for mutual friends of ours. We were both dateless and decided to keep each other company. One thing led to another and…"

My eyes told her I didn't need to hear any more of that. She skipped the remainder of their introductions and graduated to how she ended up making my husband a father.

"Our relationship didn't last long, Mrs. Rutherford," she told me. "Only ten months actually. Charlie…Charles and I agreed that a serious relationship was not in the cards for us. We decided to end our friendship abruptly, but cordially. I later discovered the reason behind our sudden split."

I hung on to her every word.

"It was you. Charles had made up his mind that he wanted to pursue you. Unlike most men, Charles wouldn't cheat on me. He was far too much of a gentleman for that. He gracefully backed out of the relationship, but managed to convince me before he did that it was something I wanted too."

She smiled wide, remembering.

"Soon after we split, I found out I was pregnant. At first, I considered having an abortion, but I quickly turned my thoughts from that. I decided to have the baby and to raise him on my own. I never told Charles about him. I knew it would just complicate things, and I didn't want Charles to feel obligated to stick with me. He'd already made it clear that it wasn't something he wanted to do. My son rarely asked about his father, but when he finally did, I told him his daddy was dead. I know it was wrong, but I didn't know what else to do. It wasn't until I found out that Charles was seriously ill that my conscience started eating away at me. I suddenly wanted my son to know his father, at least who he was and to meet with him at least once while he was still alive."

"How did you find out Charles was ill?" I asked her. "I didn't even know until recently."

"Charles and I have a mutual friend. I confided in him about my pregnancy. He kept my secret, and because you come into contact with him often, I prefer to keep his identity a secret too. I hope you understand." She told me.

I nodded my head, although the idea of someone I am in contact with knowing such private and intimate details about my life disturbs me. I'm curious. I desperately want to know who my Judas is, but that's not what's most important right now. I'm more curious about something else. "Did your son ever get to meet Charles?" I wanted to know. "Yes," she said. Her answer stunned me.

"He did?" I asked her. "And you introduced them as father and son?"

"Yes, I did," she said unapologetically.

"Although as soon as they saw each other they knew. Both of them knew the other without any words being said. Charlie Jr. is the spitting image of his daddy."

My head was spinning.

"How did Charles react?" I asked her. "What did he say? Was he happy? Shocked? Angry?"

Rita smiled. "Charles reached his hand out and took Little Charlie's in his. He hugged my boy and told him he loved him. He told him he felt there was another part of him out there. He talked to Little Charlie about how he wished he would have had the chance to know him, to see him being born, teach him to play ball, to make him a part of his life…and yours. He told Little Charlie all about you. He told him that you're the best thing that ever happened to him, of how much he loves you and he told Little Charlie that he was sure he would love you too. Charles wants you to meet Little Charlie. He told me that he wants Little Charlie to become a part of your life. It's not my intent to force something upon you that you don't want, but Charles made me promise to stop by and see you, to explain all of this and to ask you to tell his son all about him. He thought maybe you could share your memories with Little Charlie and fill him in on the times he lost out on. Charles wants you to tell Little Charlie all about him."

I put my head in my hands and cried. I wasn't sure whether or not I believed Rita Millard. It was possible she wanted something from me. Money maybe. It was possible that her son didn't even belong to Charles. How could I be sure? I hated her for laying all this on me at such a bad time.

"How do I know you're not lying? That you don't want something from me? Why have you come to me now? How do I know that you are who you say you are? That this isn't some type of cruel hoax?" I asked her.

She reached into her purse and took out a picture of herself with Charles. Her hair was shorter and she looked a tad bit younger. I studied the picture closely. Charles had his arm around her shoulders and she was holding a menu that had the name "La Nello's" on the front. The photo was taken at the engagement party she had spoken of earlier. I continued to focus on the picture. After scanning it more closely, I was stunned by what I saw. There stood my Judas right behind Charles, inconspicuously socializing in the background. Rita knew I'd discovered him. I handed her the picture. Now, I was livid.

"I made him promise not to tell Charles. I didn't want to interfere in any way with his relationship with you. Please understand that…" she started.

"I know," I continued for her. "That the two of you were protecting me. That you were allowing Charles and I a chance. What good martyrs you are."

I stood, indicating that our visit was over.

She picked up her purse and followed me to the door. "Christine," she said, "Please understand. Little Charles needs to know his daddy. Now that it's too late for Charles to be a father to his son, I'm gonna need you to help me fill my son's void."

"You need me to fix your mistake you mean," I told her. She hung her head.

"I guess you could say that," she agreed.

I answered her by opening my door and showing her the way out.

Stacey heard the door slam shut and came downstairs. "She gone?" she asked.

"Yeah," I told her. "For now anyway."

"You think she'll be back," she wanted to know.

"She'll be back." I nodded. "She didn't get what she came for." Stacey looked confused, but I didn't feel like clarifying things for her or rehashing Rita's visit. I redirected the conversation.

"You all packed?" I asked her. She would be leaving for Philadelphia today.

Her face paled. "I s'pose." She said. "I gotta stop by and see Revvy before I leave. Can you still drive me to the airport?"

"I wouldn't have it any other way," I told her while holding back tears. Stacey has come to mean so much to me. She's been like the daughter I never had. I don't know what I'm going to do without her. Not sure I'll be able to manage. She's been my backbone. She's held me up through times when I thought I'd fall. I can see why Charles treasured her so.

"So today's the day, huh?" I said to her.

"It seems like my time here has flown by. Things have been much more interesting around here this time around. Normally, when I come to visit Revvy, it's a little dull to be honest. I normally have a fair enough time with him, but nothing like what I've been through this time. I'm real glad I met you, Christine. I'm glad I met Charles too. The two of you have made such an impact in my life." Her eyes became misty. "Christine, I'm real sorry about the way I treated you when we met."

My eyes were misty now. "I'm sorry we met under the conditions we did. I hope you don't see me as an adulteress who just ignored her husband and her marriage. I feel that I've left a negative impression of myself imprinted on your heart, even if it has decreased in size. I'm not the woman you initially met. I was confused, hurt, and not thinking straight. I made some really bad choices. I loved Charles. You do know that, don't you?"

"I know that. Charles knew it too. He understood. He made me understand. He gave me the speech on how life gets more and more complicated as we grow through it." She hugged me. "Trust me, I know how you feel about your husband."

She stared at me for a moment, and then said something I never would have anticipated.

"You know what else I know?" she asked. "I know how much you love Revvy too. You want him in your life. You just feel guilty about it all. You feel like you'd betray Charles if you allowed yourself to have a life with him, but Christine, you promised to belong to Charles and to be faithful unto him until death do you part. Your promise has been fulfilled. Charles wants you to move on. He's okay with it. He gave you and Revvy his blessing. Charles spent so much of his last days worrying about you. All he wanted was to be assured that you would be able to move on after he was gone. You don't have to stop loving Charles in order to move on with your life and to love Revvy. Be happy, Christine. Mourn Charles, but don't make the rest of your life a funeral."

I couldn't say anything. I was crumbling inside. I wanted to hug Stacey, but my feet wouldn't move. My body became stiff. She realized that and advanced towards me instead. She hugged me again and I wailed…about her leaving, about Charles's dying, about Conrad, Rita, Charles Jr., about being scared to move forward. I cried about it all. Stacey held me tight and she cried too.

Chapter 22 – Christine

It's 3:17 p.m. Stacey's flight left on time. I was somewhat disappointed by that. I thought I'd have a little time to sit with her before she had to rush off and board her plane. I'm glad she convinced Conrad to join us on the ride there. Once she was out of sight, I needed another crutch. I hated to admit it, but I still wasn't able to stand on my own just yet. Besides, I needed to discuss the importance of openness and honesty with my Judas. He and I vowed that from this day forward, there would be no more secrets between us. We would forgive each other and ourselves for all the wrong that had happened between us and we vowed to be there for each other through thick and thin. Conrad informed me that one day, we would make our vows to each other official. I blushed, but held onto his hand and told him to go slow.

I drove the long way home, and stopped by Charles's grave along the way. I picked a flower and plucked a petal. On my first date with Charles, we played "I love you, I love you not." I placed one petal onto Charles's tombstone. "I love you," I told him and tossed the flower's remains. I ran my hand along his name and finally said goodbye. I wasn't telling him it was over and that I'd never see him again. I was simply saying, "God be with you till I do."

I got back into my car and headed home. I rolled the window down and let the wind blow through my free flowing hair. I popped in her CD and sang with CeCe as I drove.

Once I made it home, I attempted to cook dinner for one. I failed. I made far too much food and since I never was a big fan of leftovers, I decided to invite a couple of friends over to share my meal.

I picked up the phone and carefully dialed the number scribbled on the ripped corner of a piece of legal paper.

"Rita," I said almost in a whisper. "This is Mrs. Rutherford,…uh,…Christine. I was wondering if you and Little Charles would like to have dinner with me tonight. I've prepared a meal that's rather simple, but…well, if you don't have plans I mean and….only if you want to…I've got some things Little Charles might like to have that belonged to my husband,…to his daddy. Besides, I'd like to meet him. Tonight, I'd like to have Charles here with me."

I felt like a blubbering fool, but Rita was patient and sensitive on the other end. I could tell she was touched by my invitation.

"Are you sure Mrs.…Christine? It's not too soon?" She asked.

"No," I told her. "Now is actually the best time."

We chatted for a minute more before hanging up. She informed me that she could make it over in less than thirty minutes. That means she lives relatively close by. Surprisingly, that didn't bother me much. Instead, I got a little excited. I rushed around making sure that everything would be in order for my guests. I wanted them to be comfortable.

Once dinner was totally prepared to my satisfaction, I went upstairs, gathered some of Charles's belongings and pictures that I didn't mind parting with. I put them into a box and wrapped it neatly. I was pleased with myself and I felt a sense of freedom.

I held a picture of Charles in my hand and talked to him. I told him of my plans. I could feel him smiling. I sat near our bedroom window and waited for Rita's car to pull into my driveway.

When she made it, my heart pounded and my palms got sweaty. I looked up at the ceiling and asked God for guidance, and then I looked down at Charles's picture again and asked him for strength.

The doorbell rang and I went downstairs to answer it. Charles Jr. and Rita stood outside, both looking nervous and on edge. I smiled sincerely and invited them inside. I studied Charles Jr.'s face. It was a mini molding of my husband's. I reached out my hand and held his. It felt the way his daddy's did, soft, warm, and friendly. I led him and Rita to the dining room. The table was set.

We talked, ate, even laughed, and got to know each other a little. I asked Charles Jr. if he would mind standing by my side tomorrow when I placed his daddy's plaque on the gym that was being dedicated to him. He smiled wide and told me he wouldn't mind one bit. Rita cried a couple of blissful tears.

When God closes one door, he really does open another, but first he asks that we open our hearts. Today, I opened mine to Conrad, to Rita, and to my stepson Charles.

I looked across the table over the remains of our first family dinner. A cool breeze swept across my cheek. My eyes met with Charles Jr.'s and a smile took over my face. I was pleased that Charles and Charles Jr. were both in their Father's house.

DORINU PUBLICATIONS

Other Books by Dorinda D. E. Nusum

The Victory, the Sequel to Sins and Sacrifices
Afflicted and The Back Pew Crew

Sold at:

Barnes and Noble
Books and Company
Amazon.com
Chapters Indigo (Canada)
Brown and Company (Bermuda)
and many other stores online!

For signed copies, contact the author at:
dorinu@hotmail.com

About the Author

Dorinda D.E. Nusum is a native of Bermuda who currently resides in Dayton, OH. She is the owner and operator of DoriNu Publications, LLC, a company that was founded to assist aspiring writers in becoming published authors.

Nusum has won several awards for her published works. The most recent include The Dayton Book Expo's award for Fiction Bestseller (2010 and 2011) and the Sankofa Literary Society's Top 100 Books Award (2011).

In addition to penning novels and publishing, Nusum is an educator. She has been a teacher of English/Language Arts for over 15 years.

The author, publisher, educator, PR Associate, wife, and mother, plans to continue to write for as long as God will provide her with divine inspiration!

Dorinda D. E. Nusum

DORINU PUBLICATIONS